A letter addressed to the Abbe Raynal,

on the affairs of North America in which the mistakes in the Abbe's account of the Revolution of America, are corrected and cleared up

---

Thomas Paine

Contents

A letter addressed to the Abbe Raynal,

on the affairs of North America in which the mistakes in the Abbe's

account of the Revolution of America, are corrected and cleared up

BY

Thomas Paine

INTRODUCTION.

A London translation of an original work in French, by the Abbe Raynal, which treats of the Revolution of North America, having been reprinted in Philadelphia and other parts of the Continent, and as the distance at which the Abbe is placed from the American theatre of war and politics, has occasioned him to mistake several facts, or misconceive the causes or principles by which they were produced; the following tract, therefore, is published with a view to rectify them, and prevent even accidental errors intermixing with history, under the sanction of time and silence.

The Editor of the London edition has entitled it, "The Revolution of America, by the Abbe Raynal," and the American printers have followed the example. But I have understood, and I believe my information to be just, that the piece, which is more properly reflections on the Revolution, was unfairly purloined from the printer which the Abbe employed, or from the manuscript copy, and is only part of a larger work then in the press, or preparing for it. The person who procured it, appears to have been an Englishman; and though, in an advertisement prefixed to the London edition, he has endeavoured to gloss over the embezzlement with professions of patriotism, and to soften it with high encomiums on the author, yet the action, in any view in which it can be placed, is illiberal and unpardonable.

"In the course of his travels," says he, "the translator happily succeeded in obtaining a copy of this exquisite little piece, which has not yet made its appearance from any press." He publishes a French edition, in favour of those who will feel its eloquent reasoning more forcibly in its native language, at the same time with the following translation of it; in which he has been desirous, perhaps, in vain, that all the warmth, the grace, the strength, the dignity of the original, should not be lost. And he flatters himself, that the indulgence of the illustrious historian will not be wanting to a man who, of his own motion, has taken the liberty to give this composition to the public, "only from a strong persuasion, that this momentous argument will be useful, in a critical conjecture, to that country which he loves with an ardour that can be exceeded only by the nobler flame which burns in the bosom of the philanthropic author, for the freedom and happiness of all the countries upon earth."

This plausibility of setting off a dishonourable action, may pass for patriotism and sound principles with those who do not enter into its demerits, and whose interest is not injured, nor their happiness affected thereby. But it is more than probable, notwithstanding the declarations it contains, that the copy was obtained for the sake of profiting by the sale of a new and popular work, and that the professions are but a garb to the fraud.

It may, with propriety, be remarked, that in all countries where literature is (protected, and it never can flourish where it is not,) the works of an author are his legal property; and to treat letters in any other light than this, is to banish them from the country, or strangle them in the birth. The embezzlement from the Abbe RAYNAL was it is true, committed by one country upon another, and, therefore, shews no defect in the laws of either. But it is nevertheless a breach of civil manners and literary justice; neither can it be any apology, that because the countries are at war, literature shall be entitled to depredation[1].

But the forestalling the Abbe's publication by London editions, both in French and English, and thereby not only defrauding him, and throwing an expensive publication on his hands, by anticipating the sale, are only the smaller injuries which

---

1   The state of literature in America must one day become a subject of legislative consideration. Hitherto it hath been a disinterested volunteer in the service of the Revolution, and no man thought of Profits; but when peace shall give time and opportunity for study, the country will deprive itself of the honour and service of letters, and the improvement of science, unless sufficient laws are made to prevent depredation on literary property. It is well worth remarking, that Russia, who, but a few years ago, was scarcely known in Europe, owes a large share of her present greatness to the close attention she has paid, and the wise encouragement she has given to every branch of science and learning: and we have almost the same instance in France, in the reign of Lewis XIV.

such conduct may occasion. A man's opinions, whether written, or in thought, are his own until he pleases to publish them himself; and it is adding cruelty to injustice to make him the author of what future reflection or better information might occasion him to suppress or amend. There are declarations and sentiments in the Abbe's piece, which, for my own part, I did not expect to find, and such as himself, on a revisal, might have seen occasion to change, but the anticipated piracy effectually prevented him the opportunity, and precipitated him into difficulties, which, had it not been for such ungenerous fraud, might not have happened.

This mode of making an author appear before his time, will appear still more ungenerous, when we consider how exceedingly few men there are in any country, who can at once, and without the aid of reflection and revisal, combine warm passions with a cool temper, and the full expansion of imagination, with the natural and necessary gravity of judgment, so as to be rightly balanced within themselves, and to make a reader feel, fancy, and understand justly, at the same time. To call three powers of the mind into action at once, in a manner that neither shall interrupt, and that each shall aid and vigorate the other, is a talent very rarely possessed.

It often happens, that the weight of an argument is lost by the wit of setting it off, or the judgment disordered by an intemperate irritation of the passions: yet a certain degree of animation must be felt by the writer, and raised in the reader, in order to interest the attention; and a sufficient scope given to the imagination, to enable it to create in the mind a sight of the persons, characters, and circumstances of the subject; for without these, the judgment will feel little or no excitement to office, and its determinations be cold, sluggish, and imperfect. But if either or both of the two former are raised too high, or heated too much, the judgment will be jostled from its seat, and the whole matter, however important in itself, will diminish into a pantomime of the mind, in which we create images that promote no other purpose than amusement.

The Abbe's writings bear evident marks of that extension and rapidness of thinking, and quickness of sensation, which, of all others, require revisal, and the more particularly so, when applied to the living characters, of Nations or individuals in a state of war. The least misinformation or misconception leads to some wrong conclusion, and an error believed becomes the progenitor of others. And as the Abbe has suffered some inconveniences in France, by misstating certain circumstances of the war, and the characters of the parties therein, it becomes some apology for him, that those errors were precipitated into the world by the avarice of an ungenerous enemy.

A LETTER, *&c.*

To an Author of such distinguished reputation as the Abbe RAYNAL, it might very well become me to apologize for the present undertaking; but, as **to be right** is the first wish of philosophy, and the first principle of history, he will, I presume, accept from me a declaration of my motives, which are those of doing justice, in preference to any complimental apology, I might otherwise make.—The Abbe, in the course of his work, has in some instances extolled, without a reason, and wounded without a cause. He has given fame where it was not deserved, and withheld it where it was justly due; and appears to be so frequently in and out of temper with his subjects and parties, that few or none of them are decisively and uniformly marked.

It is yet too soon to write the history of the Revolution; and whoever attempts it precipitately, will unavoidably mistake characters and circumstances, and involve himself in error and difficulty. Things, like men are seldom understood rightly at first sight. But the Abbe is wrong even in the foundation of his work; that is, he has misconceived and misstated the causes which produced the rupture,, between England and her then colonies, and which led on, step by step, unstudied and uncontrived on the part of America, to a Revolution, which has engaged the attention, and affected the interest of Europe.

To prove this, I shall bring forward a passage, which, though placed towards the latter part of the Abbe's work, is more intimately connected with the beginning; and in which, speaking of the original cause of the dispute, he declares himself in the following manner—

"None," says he, "of those energetic causes, which have produced so many Revolutions upon the globe, existed in North-America. Neither religion nor laws had there been outraged. The blood of martyrs or patriots had not there streamed from scaffolds. Morals had not there been insulted. Manners, customs, habits, no object dear to Nations, had there been the sport of ridicule. Arbitrary power had not there torn any inhabitant from the arms of his family and his friends, to drag him to a dreary dungeon. Public order had not been there inverted. The principles of administration had not been changed there; and the maxims of Government had there always remained the same. The whole question was reduced to the knowing whether the mother country had, or had not a right to lay, directly or indirectly, a slight tax upon the colonies."

On this extraordinary passage, it may not be improper, in general terms, to remark, that none can feel like those who suffer; and that for a man to be a competent judge of the provocative, or, as the Abbe styles them, the energetic causes of the Revolution, he must have resided in America.

The Abbe, in saying that the several particulars he has enumerated did not exist in America, and neglecting to point out the particular period in which he means they did not exist, reduces thereby his declaration to a nullity by taking away all meaning from the passage.

They did not exist in 1763, and they all existed before 1776; consequently, as there was a time when they did ***not,*** and another when they ***did*** exist, the ***time when*** constitutes the essence of the fact; and not to give it, is to withhold the only evidence, which proves the declaration right or wrong, and on which it must stand or fall. But the declaration, as it now appears, uaccompanied by time, has an effect in holding out to the world, that there was no real cause for the Revolution, because it denies the existence of all those causes which are supposed to be justifiable, and which the Abbe styles energetic.

I confess myself exceedingly at a loss to find out the time to which the Abbe alludes; because, in another part of the work, in speaking of the Stamp Act, which was passed in 1764, he styles it, "An ***usurpation*** of the Americans' ***most precious and sacred rights.*** " Consequently he here admits the most energetic of all causes, that is, ***an usurpation of the most precious and sacred rights,*** to have existed in America twelve years before the Declaration of Independence, and ten years before the breaking out of hostilities.—The time, therefore, in which the paragraph is true, must be antecedent to the Stamp Act; but as at that time there was no revolution, nor any idea of one, it consequently applies without a meaning; and as it cannot, on the Abbe's own principle, be applied to any time ***after*** the Stamp Act; it is therefore a wandering solitary paragraph, connected with nothing, and at variance with every thing.

The Stamp Act, it is true, was repealed in two years after it was passed; but it was immediately followed by one of infinitely more mischievous magnitude, I mean the Declaratory Act, which asserted the right, as it was styled, of the British Parliament, " *to bind America in all cases whatsoever.* "

If, then, the Stamp Act was an "usurpation of the Americans' most precious and sacred rights," the Declaratory Act left them no rights at all; and contained the full grown seeds of the most despotic Government that ever existed in the world. It placed America not only in the lowest, but in the basest state of vassalage; because it demanded an unconditional submission in every thing, or, as the Act expresses it, *in all cases whatsoever:* and what renders this Act the more offensive, is, that it appears to have been passed as an act of mercy; truly, then, it may be said, that *the tender mercies of the wicked are cruel.*

All the original Charters from the Crown of England, under the faith of which, the adventurers from the old world settled in the new, were by this act displaced from their foundations; because, contrary to the nature of them, which was that of a compact, they were now made subject to repeal or alteration, at the mere will of one party only. The whole condition of America was thus put into the hands of the Parliament or the Ministry, without leaving to her the least right in any case whatsoever.

There is no despotism to which this iniquitous law did not extend; and though it might have been convenient, in the execution of it, to have consulted manners and habits, the principle of the act made all tyranny legal. It stopped no where. It went to every thing. It took in with it the whole life of a man, or, if I may so express it, an eternity of circumstances. It is the nature of law to require obedience, but this demanded servitude; and the condition of an American, under the operation of it, was not that of a subject, but a vassal. Tyranny has often been established *without* law, and sometimes *against* it, but the history of mankind does not produce another instance in which it has been established *by* law. It is an audacious outrage upon Civil Government, and cannot be too much exposed, in order to be sufficiently detected.

Neither could it be said after this, that the legislature of that country any longer made laws for this, but that it gave out commands; for wherein differed an Act of Parliament constructed on this principle, and operating in this manner, over an unrepresented people, from the orders of a military establishment?

The Parliament of England, with respect to America, was not septennial but *perpetual.* It appeared to the latter a body always in being. Its election or its expiration were to her the same as if its members succeeded by inheritance, or went out by death, or lived for ever, or were appointed to it as a matter of office. Therefore, for the people of England to have any just conception of the mind of America, respecting this extraordinary act, they must suppose all election and expiration in that country to cease for ever, and the present Parliament, its heirs, &c. to be perpetual; in this case, I ask, what would the most clamorous of them think, were an act to be passed, declaring the right of *such a Parliament* to bind *them* in all cases whatsover? For this word *whatsoever* would go as effectually to their *Magna Charta, Bill of Rights, Trial by Juries,* &c. as it went to the charters and forms of Government in America.

I am persuaded, that the Gentleman to whom I address these remarks, will not, after the passing this act, say, "That the *principles* of administration had not been *changed* in America, and that the maxims of Government had there been *always the same.* " For here is, in principle, a total overthrow of the whole, and not a subversion only, but an annihilation of the foundation of liberty, and absolute domination established in its stead.

The Abbe likewise states the case exceedingly wrong and injuriously, when he says, "that the *whole* question was reduced to the knowing whether the mother country had, or had not, a right to lay, directly or indirectly, a *slight* tax upon the colonies." This was *not the whole* of the question; neither was the *quantity* of the tax the object, either to the Ministry, or to the Americans. It was the principle, of which the tax made but a part, and the quantity still less, that formed the ground on which America opposed.

The tax on tea, which is the tax here alluded to, was neither more or less than an experiment to establish the practice of the Declaratory Law upon; modelled into the more fashionable phrase *of the universal supremacy of Parliament.* For, until this time, the Declaratory Law had lain dormant, and the framers of it had contented themselves with barely declaring an opinion.

Therefore the ***whole*** question with America, in the opening of the dispute, was, shall we be bound in all cases whatsoever by the British Parliament, or shall we not? For submission to the tea or tax act, implied an acknowledgement of the Declaratory Act, or, in other words, to the universal supremacy of Parliament, which, as they never intended to do, it was necessary they should oppose it, in its first stage of execution.

It is probable, the Abbe has been led into this mistake by perusing detached pieces in some of the American newspapers; for, in a case where all were interested, every one liad a right to give his opinion; and there were many who, with the best intentions, did not chuse the best, nor indeed the true ground, to defend their cause upon. They felt themselves right by a general impulse, without being able to separate, analyze, and arrange the parts.

I am somewhat unwilling to examine too minutely into the whole of this extraordinary passage of the Abbe, lest I should appear to treat it with severity; otherwise I could shew that not a single declaration is justly founded; for instance, the reviving an obsolete act of the reign of Henry the Eighth, and fitting it to the Americans, by authority of which they were to be seized and brought from America to England, and there imprisoned and tried for any supposed offences, was, in the worse sense of the words, ***to tear them by the arbitrary power of Parliament from the arms of their families and friends, and drag them not only to dreary, but distant dungeons.*** Yet this act was contrived some years before the breaking out of hostilities. And again, though the blood of martyrs and patriots had not streamed on the scaffolds, it streamed in the streets, in the massacre of the inhabitants of Boston, by the British soldiery, in the year 1770.

Had the Abbe said that the causes which produced the Revolution in America were originally ***different*** from those which produced Revolutions in other parts of the globe, he had been right. Here the value and quality of liberty, the nature of Government, and the dignity of man were known and understood, and the attachment of the Americans to these principles produced the Revolution as a natural and almost unavoidable consequence. They had no particular family to set up or pull down. Nothing of personality was incorporated with their cause. They started evenhanded with each other, and went no faster into the several stages of it, than they were driven by the unrelenting and imperious conduct of Britain. Nay, in the last act, the Declaration of Independence, they had nearly been too late; for had it not been declared at the exact time it was, I have seen no period in their affairs since, in which it could have been declared with the same effect, and probably not at all.

But the object being formed before the reverse of fortune took place, that is before the operations of the gloomy campaign of 1776, their honour, their interest, their every thing, called loudly on them to maintain it; and that glow of thought and energy of heart, which even a distant prospect of Independence inspires, gave confidence to their hopes and resolution to their conduct, which a state of dependence could never have reached. They looked forward to happier days and scenes of rest, and qualified the hardships of the campaign by contemplating the establishment of their new-born system.

If on the other hand, we take a review of what part Britain has acted, we shall find every thing which ought to make a Nation blush. The most vulgar abuse, accompanied by that species of haughtiness, which distinguishes the hero of a mob from the character of a Gentleman: it was equally as much from her manners, as from her injustice that she lost the colonies. By the latter she provoked their principles, by the former she wore out their temper; and it ought to be held out as an example to the world, to shew, how necessary it is to conduct the business of Government with civility. In short, other Revolutions may have originated in caprice, or generated in ambition; but here, the most unoffending humility was tortured into rage, and the infancy of existence made to weep.

An union so extensive, continued and determined, suffering with patience and never in despair, could not have been produced by common causes. It must be something capable of reaching the whole soul of man, and arming it with perpetual energy. In vain it is to look for precedents among the Revolutions of former ages, to find out, by comparison, the causes of this. The spring, the progress, the object, the consequences, nay the men, their habits of thinking, and all the circumstances of the country, are different. Those of other Nations are, in general, little more than the history of their quarrels. They are marked by no important character in the annals of events; mixed in the mass of general matters they occupy but a common page; and while the chief of the successful partisans stepped into power, the plundered multitude sat down and sorrowed. Few, very few of them are accompanied with reformation, either in Government or manners; many of them with the most consummate profligacy.—Triumph on the one side and misery on the other were the only events. Pains, punishments, torture, and death were made the business of mankind, until compassion, the fairest associate of the heart, was driven from its place, and the eye, accustomed to continual cruelty, could behold it without offence.

But as the principles of the present Revolution differed from those which preceded it, so likewise has the conduct of America both in Government and war. Neither the foul finger of disgrace nor the bloody hand of vengeance has hitherto put a blot upon her fame. Her victories have received lustre from a greatness of lenity; and her laws been permitted to slumber, where they might justly have awakened to punish. War, so much the trade of the world, has here been only the business of necessity; and when the necessity shall cease, her very enemies must confess, that as she drew the sword in her just defence, she used it without cruelty, and sheathed it without revenge.

As it is not my design to extend these remarks to an history, I shall now take my leave of this passage of the Abbe, with an observation, which, until something unfolds itself to convince me otherwise, I cannot avoid believing to be true;—which is, that it was the first determination of the British Cabinet to quarrel with America at all events.

They, (the members who compose the Cabinet) had no doubt of success, if they could once bring it to the issue of a battle; and they expected from a conquest what they could neither propose with decency, nor hope for by negociation. The Charters and Constitutions of the colonies were become to them matters of offence, and their rapid progress in property and population were disgustingly beheld as the growing and natural means of independence. They saw no way to retain them long, but by reducing them in time. A conquest would at once have made them both lords and landlords, and put them in possession both of the revenue and the rental. The whole trouble of Government would have ceased in a victory, and a final end been put to remonstrance and debate. The experience of the Stamp Act had taught them how to quarrel with the advantages of cover and convenience, and they had nothing to do but to renew the scene, and put contention into motion. They hoped for a rebellion and they made one. They expected a Declaration of Independence, and they were not disappointed. But, after this, they looked for victory, and gained a defeat.

If this be taken as the generating cause of the contest, then is every part of the conduct of the British Ministry-consistent, from the commencement of the dispute, until the signing the treaty of Paris, after which, conquest becoming doubtful, they retreated to negociation, and were again defeated.

Though the Abbe possesses and displays great powers of genius, and is a master of style and language, he seems not to pay equal attention to the office of an historian. His facts are coldly and carelessly stated. They neither inform the reader, nor interest him. Many of them are erroneous, and most of them defective and obscure. It is undoubtedly both an ornament and an useful addition to history, to accompany it with maxims and reflections. They afford, like-wise, an agreeable change to the style, and a more diversified manner of expression; but it is absolutely necessary that the root from whence they spring, or the foundation on which they are raised, should be well attended to, which in this work they are not. The Abbe hastens through his narrations as if he was glad to get from them, that Ire may enter the more copious field of eloquence and imagination.

The actions of Trenton and Princeton, in New Jersey, in December, 1770, and January following, on which the fate of America stood for a while, trembling on the point of suspense, and from which the most important consequences followed, are comprised within a single paragraph, faintly conceived, and barren of character, circumstance, and description.

"On the 25th of December," says the Abbe, "they (the Americans) crossed the Delaware, and fell, ***accidentally,*** upon Trenton, which was occupied by fifteen hundred of the twelve thousand Hessians, sold in so base a manner by their avaricious master, to the King of Great Britain. This corps was ***massacred,*** taken, or dispersed. Eight days after, three English regiments were, in like manner, driven from Princeton; but after having better supported their reputation than the foreign troops in their pay."

This is all the account which is given of these most interesting events. The Abbe has preceded them by two or three pages, on the military operations of both armies, from the time of General Howe arriving before New York, from Halifax, and the vast reinforcements of British and foreign troops with Lord Howe from England. But in these there is so much mistake, and so many omissions, that, to set them right, must be the business of history, and not of a letter. The action of Long-Island is but barely hinted at; and the operations at the White Plains wholly omitted: as are likewise, the attack and loss of Fort Washington, with a garrison of about two thousand five hundred men, and the precipitate evacuation of Fort Lee, in consequence thereof; which losses were, in a great measure, the cause of the retreat through the Jerseys, to the Delaware, a distance of about ninety miles. Neither is the manner of the retreat described, which, from the season of the year, the nature of the country, the nearness of the two armies, (sometimes within sight and shot of each other for such a length of way) the rear of the one employed in pulling down bridges, and the van of the other in building them up, must necessarily be accompanied with many interesting circumstances.

It was a period of distresses. A crisis rather of danger than of hope: there is no description can do it justice; and even the actors in it, looking back upon the scene, are surprised how they got through; and at a loss to account for those powers of the mind, and springs of animation, by which they withstood the force of accumulated misfortune.

It was expected, that the time for which the army was enlisted, would carry the campaign so far into winter, that the severity of the season, and the consequent condition of the roads, would prevent any material operation of the enemy, until the new army could be raised for the next year. And I mention it, as a matter worthy of attention by all future historians, that the movements of the American army, until the attack upon the Hessian post at Trenton, the 26th of December, are to be considered as operating to effect no other principal purpose than delay, and to wear away the campaign under all the disadvantages of an unequal force, with as little misfortune as possible.

But the loss of the garrison at Fort Washington, on the 16th of November, and the expiration of the time of a considerable part of the army, so early as the 30th of the same month, and which were to be followed by almost daily expirations afterwards, made retreat the only final expedient. To these circumstances, may be added, the forlorn and destitute condition of the few that remained; for the garrison at Fort Lee, which composed almost the whole of the retreat, had been obliged to abandon it so instantaneously, that every article of stores and baggage was left behind, and in this destitute condition, without tent, or blanket, and without any other utensils to dress their provisions, than what they procured by the way, they performed a march of about ninety miles, and had the address and management to prolong it to the space of nineteen days.

By this unexpected, or rather, unthought-of turn of affairs, the country was, in an instant, surprised into confusion, and found an enemy within its bowels, without an army to oppose him. There were no succours to be had, but from the free-will offering of the inhabitants. All was choice, and every man reasoned for himself.

It was in this situation of affairs, equally calculated to confound, or to inspire, that the gentleman, the merchant, the farmer, the tradesman, and the labourer, mutually turned out from all the conveniencies of home, to perform the duties of private soldiers, and undergo the severities of a winter campaign. The delay, so judiciously contrived oh the retreat, afforded time for the volunteer reinforcements to join General Washington on the Delaware.

The Abbe is likewise wrong in saying, that the American army fell, ***accidentally,*** on Trenton. It was the very object for which General Washington crossed the Delaware in the dead of night, and in the midst of snow, storms, and ice; and which he immediately re-crossed with his prisoners, as soon as he had accomplished his purpose. Neither was the intended enterprize a secret to the enemy, information having been sent of it, by letter, from a British Officer, at Princeton, to Colonel Rolle, who commanded the Hessians at Trenton, which letter was afterwards found by the Americans. Nevertheless, the post was completely surprised. A small circumstance, which had the appearance of mistake on the part of the Americans, led to a more capital and real mistake on the part of Rolle.

The case was this: A detachment of twenty or thirty Americans had been sent across the river from a post, a few miles above, by an officer unacquainted with the intended attack; these were met by a body of Hessians on the night, to which the information pointed, which was Christmas night, and repulsed. Nothing further appearing, and the Hessians mistaking this for the advanced party, supposed the enterprise disconcerted, which at that time was not began, and under this idea returned to their quarters; so that, what might have raised an alarm, and brought the Americans into an ambuscade, served to take off the force of an information, and promote the success of the enteprize. Soon after day-light General Washington entered the town and after a little opposition, made himself master of it, with upwards of nine hundred prisoners.

This combination of equivocal circumstances, falling within what the Abbe styles " ***the wide empire of chance,*** " would have afforded a fine field for thought; and I wish for the sake of that elegance of reflection he is so capable of; using, that he had known it.

But the action at Princeton was accompanied by a still greater embarrassment of matters, and followed by more extraordinary consequences. The Americans, by a happy stroke of generalship, in this instance, not only deranged and defeated all the plans of the British, in the intended moment of execution, but drew from their posts the enemy they were not able to drive, and obliged them to close the campaign. As the circumstance is a curiosity in war, and not well understood in Europe, I shall, as concisely as lean, relate the principal parts; they may serve to prevent future historians from error, and recover from forgetfulness a scene of magnificent fortitude.

Immediately after the surprise of the Hessians at Trenton, General Washington recrossed the Delaware, which at this place is about three quarters of a mile over, and re-assumed his former post on the Pennsylvania side. Trenton remained unoccupied, and the enemy were posted at Princeton, twelve miles distant, on the road towards New York. The weather was now growing very severe, and as there were very few houses near the shore where General Washington had taken his station, the greatest part of his army remained out in the woods and fields. These, with some other circumstances induced the re-crossing the Delaware, and taking possession of Trenton. It was undoubtedly a bold adventure, and carried with it the appearance of defiance, especially when we consider the panic-struck condition of the enemy on the loss of the Hessian post. But in order to give a just idea of the affair, it is necessary I should describe the place.

Trenton is situated on a rising ground, about three quarters of a mile distant from the Delaware, on the eastern or Jersey side; and is cut into two divisions by a small creek or rivulet, sufficient to turn a mill which is on it, after which, it empties itself at nearly right angles into the Delaware. The upper division, which is to the north-east, contains about seventy or eighty houses, and the lower, about forty or fifty. The ground on each side of this creek, and on which the houses are, is likewise rising, and the two divisions present an agreeableprospect to each other, with the creek between, on which there is a small stone bridge of one arch.

Scarcely had General Washington taken post here, and before the several parties of militia, out on detachments, or on their way, could be collected, than the British, leaving behind them a strong garrison at Princeton, marched suddenly, and entered Trenton at the upper or north-east quarter. A party of the Americans skirmished with the advanced party of the British, to afford time for removing the stores and baggage, and withdrawing over the bridge.

In a little time the British had possession of one half of the town, General Washington of the other, and the creek only separated the two armies. Nothing could be a more critical situation than this; and if ever the fate of America depended upon the event of a day, it was now. The Delaware was filling fast with large sheets of driving ice, and was impassable, so that no retreat into Pennsylvania could be effected, neither is it possible, in the face of an enemy, to pass a river of such extent. The roads were broken and rugged with the frost, and the main road was occupied by the enemy.

About four o'clock a party of the British approached the bridge, with a design to gain it, but were repulsed. They made no more attempts, though the creek is passable any where between the bridge and the Delaware. It runs in a rugged natural-made ditch, over which a person may pass with little difficulty, the stream being rapid and shallow. Evening was now coming on, and the British, believing they had all the advantages they could wish for, and that they could use them when they pleased, discontinued all further operations, and held themselves prepared to make the attack next morning.

But the next morning produced a scene, as elegant as it was unexpected. The British were under arms and ready to march to action, when one of their light-horse from Princeton came furiously down the street, with an account that General Washington had that morning attacked and carried the British post at that place, and was proceeding on to seize the magazine at Brunswick; on which the British, who were then on the point of making an assault on the evacuated camp of the Americans, wheeled about, and in a fit of consternation marched for Princeton.

This retreat is one of those extraordinary circumstances, that in future ages may probably pass for fable. For it will with difficulty be believed that two armies, on which such important consequences depended, should be crowded into so small a space as Trenton; and that the one, on the eve of an engagement, when every ear is supposed to be open, and every watchfulness employed, should move completely from the ground, with all its stores, baggage and artillery, unknown and even unsuspected by the other. And so entirely were the British deceived, that when they heard the report of the cannon and small arms at Princeton, they supposed it to be thunder, though in the depth of winter.

General Washington, the better to cover and disguise his retreat from Trenton, had ordered a line of fires to be lighted up in front of his camp. These not only served to give art appearance of going to rest, and continuing that deception, but they effectually concealed from the British whatever; was acting behind them, for flame can no more be seen, through than a wall, and in this situation, it may with some propriety be said, they became a pillar of fire to the one army, and a pillar of cloud to the other: after this, by a circuitous march of about eighteen miles, the Americans reached Princeton early in the morning.

The number of prisoners taken were between two and three hundred, with which General Washington immediately set off. The van of the British army from Trenton entered Princeton about an hour after the Americans had left it, who, continuing their march for the remainder of the day, arrived in the evening at a convenient situation, wide of the main road to Brunswick, and about sixteen miles distant from Princeton. But so wearied and exhausted were they, with the continual and unabated service and fatigue of two days and a night, from action to action, without shelter and almost without refreshment, that the bare and frozen ground, with no other covering than the sky, became to them a place of comfortable rest. By these two events, and with but little comparative force to accomplish them, the Americans closed with advantage, a campaign, which but a few days before threatened the country with destruction. The British army, apprehensive for the safety of their magazines at Brunswick, eighteen miles distant, marched immediately for that place, where they arrived late in the evening, and from which they made no attempts to move for nearly five months.

Having thus stated the principal outlines of these two most interesting actions, I shall now quit them, to put the Abbe right in his misstated account of the debt and paper money of America, wherein, speaking of these matters, he says,

"These ideal riches were rejected. The more the multiplication of them was urged by want, the greater did their, depreciation grow. The Congress was indignant at the affronts given to its money, and declared all those to be traitors to their country who should not receive it as they would have received gold itself.

"Did not this body know, that possessions are no more to be controuled than feelings are? Did it not perceive; that in the present crisis, every rational man would be afraid of exposing his fortune? Did it not see, that in the beginning of a republic it permitted to itself the exercise of such acts of despotism as are unknown even in the countries which are moulded to, and become familiar with servitude and oppression? Could it pretend that it did not punish a want of confidence with the pains which would have been scarcely merited by revolt and treason? Of all this was the Congress well aware. But it had no choice of means. Its despised and despicable scraps of paper were actually thirty times below their original value, when more of them were ordered to be made. On the 13th of September 1779, there was of this paper money, amongst the public, to the amount of £35,544,155. The state owed moreover £8,385,356, without reckoning the particular debts of single provinces."

In the above-recited passages, the Abbe speaks as if the United States had contracted a debt of upwards of forty millions of pounds sterling, besides the debts of individual States. After which, speaking of foreign trade with America, he says, that "those countries in Europe, which are truly commercial ones, knowing that North America had been reduced to contract debts at the epoch of even her greatest, prosperity, wisely thought, that in her present distress, she would be able to pay but very little, for what might be carried to her."

I know it must be extremely difficult to make foreigners understand the nature and circumstances of our paper money, because there are natives who do not understand it themselves. But with us its fate is now determined. Common consent has consigned it to rest with that kind of regard which the long service of inanimate things insensibly obtains from mankind. Every stone in the bridge, that has carried us over, seems to have a claim upon our esteem. But this was a corner-stone, and its usefulness cannot be forgotten. There is something in a grateful mind, which extends itself even to things that can neither be benefitted by regard, nor suffer by neglect: But so it is; and almost every man is sensible of the effect.

But to return. The paper money, though issued from Congress under the name of dollars, did not come from that body always at that value. Those which were issued the first year, were equal to gold and silver. The second year less; the third still less; and so on, for nearly the space of five years; at the end of which, I imagine, that the whole value at which Congress might pay away the several emissions, taking them together, was about ten or twelve millions of pounds sterling.

Now, as it would have taken ten or twelve millions sterling of taxes, to carry on the war for five years, and, as while this money was issuing and likewise depreciating down to nothing, there were none, or few valuable taxes paid; consequently the event, to the public was the same, whether they sunk ten or twelve millions of expended money, by depreciation, or paid ten or twelve millions by taxation; for as they did not do both, and chose to do one, the matter, in a general view, was indifferent. And therefore, what the Abbe supposes to be a debt, has now no existence; it having been paid, by every body consenting to reduce it, at his own expence, from the value of the bills continually passing among themselves, a sum, equal to nearly what the expence of the war was for five years.

Again.—The paper money having now ceased, and the depreciation with it, and gold and silver supplied its place, the war will now be carried on by taxation, which will draw from the public a considerable less sum than what the depreciation drew; but as, while they pay the former, they do not suffer the latter, and as, when they suffered the latter, they did not pay the former, the thing will be nearly equal, with this moral advantage, that taxation occasions frugality and thought, and depreciation produced dissipation and carelessness.

And again.—If a man's portion of taxes conies to less than what he lost by the depreciation, it proves the alteration is in his favour. If it comes to more, and he is justly assessed, it shews that he did not sustain his proper share of depreciation, because the one was as operatively his tax as the other.

It is true, that it never was intended, neither was it fore seen, that the debt contained in the paper currency should sink itself in this manner; but as by the voluntary conduct of all and of every one it is arrived at this fate, the debt in paid by those who owed it. Perhaps nothing was ever so universally the act of a country as this. Government had no hand in it. Every man depreciated his own money by his own consent, for such was the effect which the raising the nominal value of goods produced. But as by such reduction he sustained a loss equal to what he must have paid to sink it by taxation, therefore the line of justice is to consider his loss by the depreciation as his tax for that time, and not to tax him when the war is over, to make that money good in any other person's hand, which became, nothing in his own.

Again.—The paper currency was issued for the express purpose of carrying on the war. It has performed that service, without any other material change to the public, while it lasted. But to suppose, as some did, that at the end of the war, it was to grow into gold and silver, or become equal thereto, was to suppose that we were to *get* two hundred millions of dollars by *going to war,* instead of *paying* the cost of carrying it on.

But if any thing in the situation of America, as to her currency or her circumstances, yet remains not understood; then let it be remembered, that this war is the public's war; the people's war; the country's war. It is *their* independence that is to be supported; *their* property that is to be secured; *their* country that is to be saved. Here, Government, the army and the people, are mutually and reciprocally one. In other wars, kings may lose their thrones and their dominions; but here, the loss must fall on the *majesty of the multitude,* and the property they are contending to save. Every man being sensible of this, he goes to the field, or pays his portion of the charge as the Sovereign of his own possessions; and when he is conquered a monarch falls.

The remark which the Abbe, in the conclusion of the passage, has made respecting America contracting debts in the time of her prosperity (by which he means, before the breaking out of hostilities), serves to shew, though he has not made the application, the very great commercial difference between a dependent and an independent country. In a state of dependence, and with a fettered commerce, though with all the advantages of peace, her trade could not balance itself, and she annually run into debt. But now, in a state of independence, though involved in war, she requires no credit; her stores are full of merchandise, and gold and silver are become the currency of the country. How these things have established themselves, it is difficult to account for: but they are facts, and facts are more powerful than arguments.

As it is probable this letter will undergo a republication in Europe, the remarks here thrown together will serve to shew the extreme folly of Britain, in resting her hopes of success on the extinction of our paper currency. The expectation is at once so childish and forlorn, that it places her in the laughable condition of a famished lion watching for prey at a spider's web.

From this account of the currency, the Abbe proceeds to stale the condition of America in the winter 1777, and the spring following; and closes his observations with mentioning the treaty of alliance, which was signed in France, and the propositions of the British Ministry, which were rejected in America. But in the manner in which the Abbe has arranged his facts, there is a very material error, that not only he, but other European historians, have fallen into: none of them have assigned the true cause why the British proposals were rejected, and all of them have assigned a wrong one.

In the winter 1777, and the spring following, Congress were assembled at York-town in Pennsylvania, the British were in possession of Philadelphia, and General Washington with the army were encamped in huts at the Valley-Forge, twenty-five miles distant therefrom. To all who can remember it, it was a season of hardship, but not of despair; and the Abbe, speaking of this period and its inconveniencies, says,

"A multitude of privations, added to so many other misfortunes, might make the Americans regret their former tranquillity, and incline them to an accommodation with England. In vain, had the people been bound to the new Government, by the sacredness of oaths, and the influence of religion. In vain, had endeavours been used to convince them, that it was impossible to treat safely, with a country, in which one Parliament might overturn what should have been established by another. In vain, had they been threatened with the eternal resentment of an exasperated and vindictive enemy. It was possible that these distant troubles might not be balanced by the weight of present evils.

"So thought the British Ministry, when they sent to the New World, public agents, authorised to offer every thing, except independence, to these very Americans, from whom they had, two years before, exacted an unconditional submission. It is not improbable, but that, by this plan of conciliation, a few months sooner, some effect might have been produced. But at the period at which it was proposed by the Court of London, it was rejected with disdain, because, this method appeared but as an argument of fear, and wickedness. The people were already re-assured.

The Congress, the Generals, the troops, the bold and skilful men in each colony, had possessed themselves of the authority; every thing had recovered its first spirit. ***This was the effect of a treaty of friendship and commerce between the United States, and the Court of Versailles, signed, the 6th of February,*** 1778."

On this passage of the Abbe's, I cannot help remarking, that, to unite time with circumstance, is a material nicety in history; the want of which, frequently throws it into endless confusion and mistake, occasions a total separation between causes, and consequences, and connects them with others they are not immediately, and, sometimes, not at all related to.

The Abbe, in saying that the offers of the British Ministry, "were rejected with disdain," is ***right*** as to the ***fact,*** but ***wrong*** as to the ***time;*** and the error in the time, has occasioned him to be mistaken in the cause.

The signing the treaty of Paris, the 6th of February, 1778, could have no effect on the mind or politics of America, until it was ***known in America;*** and, therefore, when the Abbe says, that the rejection of the British offers was in consequence of the alliance, he must mean, that it was in consequence of the alliance ***being known*** in America; which was not the case: and, by this mistake, he not only takes from her the reputation, which her unshaken fortitude, in that trying situation, deserves, but is likewise led very injuriously to suppose that had she ***not known*** of the treaty, the offers would probably have been accepted; whereas, she knew nothing of the treaty at the time of the rejection, and consequently, did not reject them on that ground.

The propositions or offers abovementioned, were contained in two bills, brought into the British Parliament, by Lord North, on the 17th of February, 1778. Those bills were hurried through both Houses with unusual haste; and before they had gone through all the customary forms of Parliament, copies of them were sent over to Lord Howe, and General Howe, then in Philadelphia, who were likewise Commissioners. General Howe ordered them to be printed in Philadelphia, and sent copies of them, by a flag, to General Washington, to be forwarded to Congress, at York Town, where they arrived the 21st of April, 1778. Thus much for the arrival of the bills in America.

Congress, as is their usual mode, appointed a committee from their own body, to examine them, and report thereon. The report was brought in the next day, (the twenty-second) was read, and unanimously agreed to, entered on their, journals, and published for the information of the country. Now this report must be the rejection to which the Abbe alludes, because Congress gave no other formal opinion on those bills and propositions: and on a subsequent application from the British Commissioners, dated, the 27th of May, and received at York Town, the 6th of June, Congress immediately referred them for answer, to their printed resolves of the 22d of April.—Thus much for the rejection of the offers.

On the 2d of May, that is, eleven days after the above rejection, was made, the treaty between the United States, and France, arrived at York Town and, until this moment, Congress had not the least notice or idea that such a measure was in any train of execution. But lest this declaration of mine should pass only for assertion, I shall support it by proof, for it is material to tile character and principle of the Revolution, to shew, that no condition of America, since the Declaration of Independence, however trying, and severe, ever operated to produce the most distant idea of yielding it up, either by force, distress, artifice, or persuasion. And this proof is the more necessary, because it was the system of the British Ministry, at this time, as well as before, and since, to hold out to the European powers, that America was unfixed in her resolutions and policy; hoping, by this artifice, to lessen her reputation in Europe, and weaken the confidence which those powers, or any of them, might be inclined to place in her.

At the time these matters were transacting, I was Secretary to the foreign department of Congress. All the political letters from the American Commissioners, rested in my hands, and all that were officially written, went from my office: and so far from Congress knowing any thing of the signing the treaty, at the time they rejected the British offers, they had not received a line of information from their Commissioners at Paris, on any subject whatever, for upwards of a twelvemonth. Probably, the loss of the port of Philadelphia, and the navigation of the Delaware, together with the danger of the seas, covered, at this time, with British cruizers, contributed to the disappointment.

One packet, it is true, arrived at York Town, in January preceding, which was about three months before the arrival of the treaty, but, strange as it may appear, every letter had been taken out, before it was put on board the vessel which brought it from France, and blank white paper put in their stead.

Having thus stated the time when the proposals from the British Commissioners were first received, and likewise the time when the treaty of alliance arrived, and shewn that the rejection of the former was eleven days, prior to the arrival of the latter, and without the least knowledge of such circumstance having taken place, or being about to take place; the rejection, therefore, must, and ought to be attributed to the first unvaried sentiments of America, respecting the enemy she is at war with, and her determination to support her independence to the last possible effort, and not to any new circumstance in her favour, which, at that time, she did not, and could not, know of.

Besides, there is a vigour of determination, and spirit of defiance, in the language of the rejection, (which I here sub-join) which derive their greatest glory, by appearing before the treaty was known; for that, which is bravery in distress, becomes insult in prosperity. And the treaty placed America on such a strong foundation, that had she then known it, the answer which she gave, would have appeared rather as an air of triumph, than as the glowing serenity of fortitude.

Upon the whole, the Abbe appears to have entirely mistaken the matter; for instead of attributing the rejection of the propositions, to our knowledge of the treaty of alliance, he should have attributed the origin of them in the British Cabinet, to their knowledge of that event. And then the reason why they were hurried over to America, in the state of bills, that is, before they were passed into acts, is easily accounted for; which is, that they might have the chance of reaching America before any knowledge of the treaty should arrive, which they were lucky enough to do, and there met the fate they so richly merited. That these bills were brought into the British Parliament, after the treaty with France was signed, is proved from the dates: the treaty being on the 6th, and the bills on the 17th, of February. And that the signing the treaty was known in Parliament, when the bills were brought in, is likewise proved by a speech of Mr. Charles Fox, on the said 17th, of February, who, in reply to Lord North, informed the House of the treaty being signed, and challenged the Minister's knowledge of the same fact[2].

"THE Committee to whom was referred the General's letter of the 18th, containing a certain printed paper sent from Philadelphia, purporting to be the draught of a Bill for declaring the intentions of the Parliament of Great Britain, as to the

2   IN CONGRESS, April 22d, 1778.

exercise of what they are pleased to term their right of imposing taxes within these United States; and also the draft of a Bill to enable the King of Great Britain to appoint Commissioners, with powers to treat, consult, and agree upon the means of quieting certain disorders within the said States, beg leave to observe,

"That the said paper being industriously circulated by emissaries of the enemy, in a partial and secret manner, the same ought to be forthwith printed for the public information.

"The Committee cannot ascertain whether the contents of the said paper have been framed in Philadelphia or in Great Britain, much less whether the same are really and truly intended to be brought into the Parliament of that kingdom, or whether the said Parliament will confer thereon the usual solemnities of their laws. But are inclined to believe this will happen, for the following reasons:

"1st. Because their General hath made divers feeble efforts to set on foot some kind of treaty during the last winter, though either from a mistaken idea of his own dignity and importance, the want of information, or some other cause, he hath not made application to those who are invested with proper authority.

"2dly. Because they suppose that the fallacious idea of a cessation of hostilities will render these States remiss in their preparations of war.

"3dly. Because believing the Americans wearied with war, they suppose we will accede to the terms for the sake of peace.

"4thly. Because they suppose that our negociations may be subject to a like corrupt influence with their debates.

"5thly. Because they expect from this step the same effects they did from what one of their Ministers thought proper to call his ***conciliatory motion,*** viz. that it will prevent foreign powers from giving aid to these States; that it will lead their own subjects to continue a little longer the present war; and that it will detach some weak men in America from the cause of freedom and virtue.

"6thly. Because their King, from his own shewing, hath reason to apprehend that his fleets and armies, instead of being employed against the territories of these States, will be necessary for the defence of his own dominions. And,

"7thly. Because the impracticability of subjugating this country, being every day more and more manifest, it is their interest to extricate themselves from the war upon any terms.

"The Committee beg leave further to observe, That, upon a supposition, the matters contained on the said paper will really go 'into the British Statute Book, they serve to shew, in a clear point of view, the weakness and wickedness of the enemy.

"THEIR WEAKNESS.

"1st. Because they formerly declared, not only that they had a right to bind the inhabitants of these States in all cases whatsoever/but also, that the said inhabitants should *absolutely* and *unconditionally* submit to the exercise of that right. And this submission they have endeavoured to exact by the sword. Receding from this claim, therefore; under the present circumstances, shews their inability to enforce it.

"2dly. Because their Prince hath heretofore rejected the humblest petitions of the Representatives of America, praying to be considered as subjects, and protected in the enjoyment of peace, liberty, and safety; and hath waged a most cruel war against them, and employed the savages to butcher innocent women and children. But now the same Prince pretends to treat with those very Representatives, and grant to the arms of America what he refused to her prayers.

"3dly. Because they have uniformly laboured to conquer this continent, rejecting every idea of accommodation proposed to them, from a confidence in their own strength. Wherefore it is evident, from the change in their mode of attack, that they have lost this confidence. And,

"4thly. Because the constant language, spoken not only by their Ministers, but by the most public and authentic act of the Nation, hath been, that it is incompatible with their dignity to treat with the Americans while they have arms in their hands. Notwithstanding which, an offer is now about to be made for treaty.

"The wickedness and insincerity of the enemy appear from the following considerations:

"1st. Either the Bills now to be passed contain a direct or indirect cession of a part of their former claims, or they do not. If they do, then it is acknowledged that they have sacrificed many brave men in an unjust quarrel. If they do not, then they are calculated to deceive America into terms, to which neither argument before the war, nor force since, could procure her assent.

"2dly. The first of these Bills appears, from the title, to be a declaration of the

intentions of the British Parliament concerning the exercise of the right of imposing taxes within these States. Wherefore, should these States treat under the said
Bill, they would indirectly acknowledge that right, to obtain which acknowledgment the present war hath been avowedly undertaken and prosecuted on the part
of Great Britain.

"3dly. Should such pretended right he so acquiesced in, then of consequence
the same might be exercised whenever the British Parliament should find themselves in a different temper and disposition; since it must depend upon those, and
such like contingencies, how far men will act according to their former intentions.

"4thly. The said first Bill, in the body thereof, containeth no new matter, but
is precisely the same with the motion before mentioned, and liable to all the objections which lay against the said motion, excepting the following particular, viz. that
by the motion, actual taxation was to be suspended, so long as America should give
as much as the said Parliament might think proper: whereas, by the proposed Bill,
it is to be suspended as long as future Parliaments continue of the same mind with
the present.

"4thly. From the second Bill it appears, that the British King may, if he pleases,
appoint Commissioners to treat and agree with those whom they please, about a
variety of things therein mentioned. But such treaties and agreements are to be of
no validity without the concurrence of the said Parliament, except so far as they
relate to the suspension of hostilities, and of certain of their acts, the grunting of
pardons, and the appointment of Governors to these Sovereign, free, and independent States. Wherefore, the laid Parliament nave reserved to themselves in express
words, the power of setting aside any such treaty, and taking tire advantage of any
circumstances which may arise to subject this continent to their usurpations.

"6thly. The said Bill, by holding forth a tender of pardon, implies a criminality
in our justifiable resistance, and consequently, to treat under it, would be an implied acknowledgment,-that the inhabitants of these States were, what Britain has
declared them to be,—Rebels.

"7thly. The inhabitants of these States being claimed by them as subjects, they
may infer, from the nature of the negociation now pretended to be set on foot,
that the said inhabitants would, of right be afterwards bound by such laws as they
should make. Wherefore any agreement entered into on such negociation might at

any future time be repealed. And,

"8thly. Because the said Bill purports, that the Commissioners therein mentioned may treat with private individuals; a measure highly derogatory to the dignity of the National character.

"From all which it appears evident to your Committee, that the said Bills are intended to operate upon the hopes and fears of the good people of these States, so as to create divisions among them, and a defection from the common cause, now by the blessing of Divine Providence drawing near to a favourable issue. That they are the sequel of that insidious plan, which, from the days of the Stamp-act down to the present time, hath involved this country in contention and bloodshed. And that as ill other cases so in this, although circumstances may force them at times to recede from their unjustifiable claims, there can be no doubt but they will as heretofore, upon the first favourable occasion, again display that lust of domination, which hath rent in twain the mighty empire of Britain.

"Upon the whole matter, the Committee beg leave to report it as their opinion, That the Americans united in this arduous contest upon principles of common interest, for the defence of common rights and privileges, which union hath been cemented by common calamities, and by mutual good offices and affection, so the great cause for which they contend, and in which all mankind are interested, must derive its success from the continuance of that union. Wherefore any man or body of men, who should presume to make any separate or partial convention or agreement with Commissioners under the Crown of Great Britain, or any of them, ought to be considered and treated as open and avowed enemies of these United States.

"And further, your Committee beg leave to report it as their opinion, That these United States cannot, with propriety hold any conference or treaty with any Commissioners on the part of Great Britain, unless they shall, as a preliminary thereto, either withdraw their fleets and admirals, or else, in positive pr express terms, acknowledge the Independence of the said States.

"And inasmuch as it appears to be the design of the enemies of these States to lull them into a fatal security—to the end that they may act with a becoming weight and importance, it is the opinion of your Committee, That the several States be called upon to use the most strenuous exertions to have their respective quotas of continental troops in the field as soon as possible, and that all the militia of the said States be held in readiness, to act as occasion may require."

The following is the answer of Congress to the second application of the Commissioners.

York Town, June 6, 1778.

"SIR,

"I HAVE had the honour of laying your letter of the 3d instant, with the acts of the British Parliament, which came in-closed, before Congress; and I am instructed to acquaint you, Sir, that they have already expressed their sentiments upon bills not essentially different from those acts, in a publication of the 22d of April last.

"Be assured, Sir, when the King of Great Britain shall be seriously disposed to put an end to the unprovoked and cruel war waged against these United States, Congress will readily attend to such terms of peace, as may consist with the honour of independent Nations, the interest of their constituents, and the sacred regard they mean to pay to treaties. I have the honour to be, Sir,

Your most obedient, and most humble servant, HENRY LAURENS, President of Congress."

"His Excellency, "Sir Henry Clinton, K. B. Philadelphia]

Though I am not surprised to see the Abbe mistake in matters of history, acted at so great a distance from his sphere of immediate observation, yet I am more than surprised to find him wrong, (or, at least, what appears so to me) in the well-enlightened field of philosophical reflection. Here the materials are his own; created by himself; and the error, therefore, is an act of the mind. Hitherto, my remarks have been confined to circumstances; the order in which they arose, and the events they produced. In these, my information being better than the Abbe's, my task was easy. How I may succeed in controverting matters of sentiment and opinion, with one whom years, experience, and long established reputation have placed in a superior line, lam less confident in; bur, as they fall within the scope of my observations, it would be improper to pass them over.

From this part of the Abbe's work to the latter end, I find several expressions which appear to me to start, with a cynical complexion, from the path of liberal thinking; or at least, they are so involved, as to lose many of the beauties which distinguish other parts of the performance.

The Abbe having brought his work to the period when the treaty of alliance

between France, and the United States commenced, proceeds to make some remarks thereon.

"In short," says he, "philosophy, whose first sentiment is the desire to see all
governments just, and all people happy, in casting her eyes upon this alliance of a
monarchy, with a people who are defending their liberty, *is curious to know its
motive. She sees, at once, too clearly, that the happiness of mankind has no part
in it.* "

Whatever train of thinking or of temper the Abbe might be in, when he penned
this expression, matters not. They will neither qualify the sentiment, nor add to its
defect. If right, it needs no apology; if wrong, it merits no excuse. It is sent into the
world as an opinion of philosophy, and may be examined without regard to the
author.

It seems to be a defect, connected with ingenuity, that it often employs itself
more in matters of curiosity than usefulness. Man must be the privy counsellor of
fate, or something is not right. He must know the springs, the whys and wherefores
of every thing, or he sits down unsatisfied. Whether this be a crime, or only a caprice of humanity, I am not enquiring into. I shall take the passage as I find it, and
place my objection against it.

It is not so properly the *motives* which *produced* the alliance, as the *consequences* which are to be *produced from it,* that mark out the field of philosophical reflection. In the one we only penetrate into the barren cave of secrecy, where
little can be known, and every thing may be misconceived; in the other, the mind
is presented with a wide extended prospect of vegetative good, and sees a thousand
blessings budding into existence.

But the expression, even within the compass of the Abbe's meaning, sets out
with an error, because it is made to declare that, which no man has authority to
declare. Who can say that the happiness of mankind made *no part of the motives*
which produced the alliance? To be able to declare this, a man must be possessed of
the mind of all the parties concerned, and know that their motives were something
else.

In proportion as the independence of America became contemplated and understood, the local advantages of it to the immediate actors, and the numerous ben-
efits it promised to mankind, appeared to be every day encreasing, and we saw not

a temporary good for the present race only, but a continued good to all posterity; these motives, therefore, added to those which preceded them, became the motives, on the part of America, which led her to propose and agree to the treaty of alliance, as the best effectual method of extending and securing happiness; and therefore, with respect to us, the Abbe is wrong.

France, on the other hand, was situated very differently to America. She was not acted upon by necessity to seek a friend, and therefore her motive in becoming one, has the strongest evidence of being good, and that which is so, must have some happiness for its object. With regard to herself she saw a train of conveniences worthy her attention. By lessening the power of an enemy, whom, at the same time she sought neither to destroy nor distress, she gained an advantage without doing an evil, and created to herself a new friend by associating with a country in misfortune. The springs of thought that lead to actions of this kind, however political they may be, are nevertheless naturally beneficent; for in all causes, good or bad, it is necessary there should be a fitness in the mind, to enable it to act in character with the object: Therefore, as a bad cause cannot be prosecuted with a good motive, so neither can a good cause be long supported by a bud one, as no man acts without a motive, therefore, in the present instance, as they cannot be bad, they must be admitted to be good. But the Abbe sets out upon such an extended scale, that he overlooks the degrees by which it is measured, and rejects the beginning of good, because the end comes not at once.

It is true that bad motives may in some degree be brought to support a good cause, or prosecute a good object; but it never continues long, which is not the case with France; for either the object will reform the mind, or the mind corrupt the object, or else, not being able, either way, to go into unison, they will separate in disgust: And this natural, though unperceived progress of association or contention between the mind and the object, is the secret cause of fidelity or defection. Every object a man pursues is, for the time, a kind of mistress to his mind: if both are good or bad, the union is natural; but if they are in reverse, and neither can seduce nor yet reform the other, the opposition grows into dislike, and a separation follows.

When the cause of America first made her appearance on the stage of the universe, there were many who, in the style of adventurers and fortune-hunters, were dangling in her train arid making their court to her with every profession of honour and attachment. They were loud in her praise, and ostentatious in her service. Every place echoed with their ardour or their anger, and they seemed like men in love. But, alas, they were fortune-hunters. Their expectations were excited, but their minds were unimpressed; and finding her not to their purpose, nor themselves reformed by her influence, they ceased their suit, and in some instances deserted and betrayed her.

There were others, who at first beheld her with indifference, and unacquainted with her character were cautious of her company. They treated her as one, who, under the fair name of liberty, might conceal the hideous figure of anarchy, or the gloomy monster of tyranny. They knew not what she was. If fair, she was fair indeed. But still she was suspected, and though born among us appeared to be a stranger.

Accident with some, and curiosity with others, brought on a distant acquaintance. They ventured to look at her. They felt an inclination to speak to her. One intimacy led to another, till the suspicion wore away, and a change of sentiment stole gradually upon the mind; and having no self-interest to serve, no passion of dishonour to gratify, they became enamoured of her innocence, and unaltered by misfortune or uninflamed by success shared with fidelity in the varieties of her fate.

This declaration of the Abbe's, respecting motives, has led me unintendedly into a train of metaphysical reasoning; but there was no other avenue by which it could so properly be approached. To place presumption against presumption, assertion against assertion, is a mode of opposition that has no effect; and therefore the more eligible method was, to shew that the declaration does not correspond with the natural progress of the mind, and the influence it has upon our conduct.—I shall now quit this part, and proceed to what! have before stated, namely, that it is not so properly the motives which produced the alliance, as the consequences to be produced from it, that mark out the field of philosophical reflections.

It is an observation I have already made in some former publication, that the circle of civilization is yet incomplete. A mutuality of wants has formed the individuals of each country into a kind of national society; and here the progress of civilization has stopped. For it is easy to see, that Nations with regard to each other (notwithstanding the ideal civil law, which every one explains as it suits him), are like individuals in a state of nature. They are regulated by no fixed principle, governed by no compulsive law, and each does independently what it pleases, or what it can.

Were it possible we could have known the world when in a state of barbarism, we might have concluded, that it never could be brought into the order we now see it. The untamed mind was then as hard, if not harder to work upon in its individual state, than the national mind is in its present one." Yet we have seen the accomplishment of the one, why then should we doubt that of the other?

There is a greater fitness in mankind to extend and complete the civilization of nations with each other at this day, than there was to begin it with the unconnected individuals at first; in the same manner that it is somewhat easier to put together the materials of a machine after they are formed, than it was to form them from original matter. The present condition of the world differing so exceedingly from what it formerly was, has given a new cast to the mind of man, more than what he appears to be sensible of. The wants of the individual, which first produced the idea of society, are now augmented into the wants of the Nation, and he is obliged to seek from another country what before he sought from the next person.

Letters, the tongue of the world, have in some measure brought all mankind acquainted, and, by an extension of their uses, are every day promoting some new friendship. Through them distant Nations become capable of conversation, and losing by degrees the awkwardness of strangers, and the moroseness of suspicion, they learn to know and understand each other. Science, the partisan of no country, but the beneficent patroness of all, has liberally opened a temple where all may meet. Her influence on the mind, like the sun on the chilled earth, has long been preparing it for higher cultivation and further improvement. The philosopher of one country sees not an enemy in the philosopher of another: he takes his seat in the temple of science, and asks not who sits beside him.

This was not the condition of the barbarian world. Then the wants of man were few, and the objects within his reach. While he could acquire these, he lived in a state of individual independence, the consequence of which, was, there was as many Nations as persons, each contending with the other, to secure something which he had, or to obtain something which he had not. The world had, then, no business to follow, no studies to exercise the mind. Their time were divided between sloth and fatigue. Hunting, and war, were their chief occupations; sleep and food their principal enjoyments.

Now, it is otherwise. A change in the mode of life haft made it necessary to to be busy; and man finds a thousand things to do now, which before he did not. Instead of placing his idea of greatness in the rude achievements of the savage, he studies arts, science, argriculture, and commerce; the refinements of the gentleman, the principles of society, and the knowledge of the philosopher.

There are many things which, in themselves, are morally, neither good nor bad, but they are productive of consequences, which are strongly marked with one or other of these characters. Thus commerce, though, in itself, a moral nullity, has had a considerable influence in tempering the human mind. It was the want of ob-jects, in the ancient world, which occasioned in them, such a rude and perpetual turn for war. Their time hung on their hands without the means of employment. The indolence they lived in, afforded leisure for mischief, and being all idle at once, and equal in their circumstances, they were easily provoked, or induced to action.

But the introduction of commerce furnished the world with objects, which, in their extent, reach every man, and give him something to think about, and some-thing to do; by these, his attention is mechanically drawn from the pursuits which a state of indolence, and an unemployed mind occasioned; and he trades with the same countries, which former ages, tempted by their productions, and too indolent to purchase them, would have gone to war with.

Thus, as I have already observed, the condition of the world being materially changed by the influence of science and commerce, it is put into a fitness, not only to admit of, but to desire an extension of civilization. The principal, and almost only remaining enemy it now has to encounter, is, *Prejudice;* for it is evidently the interest of mankind to agree, and make the best of life. The world has undergone its divisions of empire, the several boundaries of which are known and settled. The idea of conquering countries, like the Greeks and Romans, does not now exist; and experience has exploded the notion of going to war for the sake of profit. In short, the objects for war are exceedingly diminished, and there is now left scarcely any thing to quarrel about, but what arises from that demon of society, Prejudice, and the consequent sullenness and untractableness of the temper.

There is something exceedingly curious in the constitution, and operation of prejudice. It has the singular ability of accommodating itself to all the possible varieties of the human mind. Some passions and vices are but thinly scattered among mankind, and find only here and there a fitness of reception. But prejudice, like the spider, makes every where its home. It has neither taste nor choice of place, and all that it requires is room. There is scarcely a situation, except fire or water, in which a spider will not live. So, let the mind be as naked as the walls of an empty and forsaken tenement, gloomy as a dungeon, or ornamented with the richest abilities of thinking; let it be hot, cold, dark, or light; lonely or inhabited, still prejudice, if undisturbed, will fill it with cobwebs, and live, like the spider, where there seems nothing to live on. If the one prepares her food by poisoning it to her palate and her use, the other does the same; and as several of our passions are strongly charactered by the animal world, prejudice may be denominated the spider of the mind.

Perhaps no two events ever united so intimately and forcibly to combat and expel prejudice, as the Revolution of America, and the Alliance with France. Their effects are felt, and their influence already extends, as well to the old world, as the new. Our style and manner of thinking, have undergone a revolution, more extraordinary than the political revolution of the country. We see with other eyes; we hear with other ears; and think with other thoughts, than those we formerly used. We can look back on our own prejudices, as if they had been the prejudices of other people. We now see and know they were prejudices, and nothing else; and relieved from their shackles, enjoy a freedom of mind we felt not before. It was not all the argument, however powerful, nor all the reasoning, however elegant, that could have produced this change, so necessary to the extension of the mind, and the cordiality of the world, without the two circumstances of the Revolution and the Alliance.

Had America dropped quietly from Britain, no material change in sentiment had taken place. The same notions, prejudices, and conceits, would have governed in both countries, as governed them before; and, still the slaves of error and education, they would have travelled on in the beaten tract of vulgar and habitual thinking. But brought about by the means it has been, both with regard to ourselves, to France, and to England, every corner of the mind is swept of its cobwebs, poison, and dust, and made fit for the reception of generous happiness.

Perhaps there never was an alliance on a broader basis, than that between

America and France, and the progress of it is worth attending to. The countries had been enemies, not properly of themselves, but through the medium of England. They, originally, had no quarrel with each other, nor any cause for one, but what arose from the interest of England, and her arming America against France. At the same time, the Americans, at a distance from, and unacquainted with the world, and tutored in all the prejudices which governed those who governed them, conceived it their duty to act as they were taught. In doing this, they expended their substance to make conquests, not for themselves, but for their masters, who, in return, treated them as slaves.

A long succession of insolent severity, and the separation finally occasioned, by the commencement of hostilities, at Lexington, on the 19th of April, 1775, naturally produced a new disposition of thinking. As the mind closed itself towards England, it opened itself towards the world; and our prejudices, like our oppressions, underwent, though less observed, a mental examination; until we found the former as inconsistent with reason, and benevolence, as the latter were repugnant to our civil and political rights.

While we were thus advancing, by degrees, into the wide field of extended humanity, the alliance with France was concluded; an alliance not formed for the mere purpose of a day, but on just and generous grounds, and with equal, and mutual advantages; and the easy, affectionate manner in which the parties have since communicated, has made it an alliance, not of Courts only, but of countries. There is now an union of mind as well as of interest; and our hearts, as well as our prosperity, call on us to support it.

The People of England not having experienced this change, and, likewise no idea of it, they were hugging to their bosoms, the same prejudices we were trampling beneath our feet; and they expected to keep a hold upon America, by that narrowness of thinking which America disdained. What they were proud of, we dispised; and this is a principle cause why all their negociations, constructed on this ground, have failed. We are now, really, another people, and cannot again go back to ignorance and prejudice. The mind once enlightened, cannot again become dark. There is no possibility, neither is there any term, to express the supposition by, of the mind unknowing any thing it already knows; and, therefore, all attempts on the part of England, fitted to the former habit of America, and on the expectation of their applying now, will be like persuading a seeing man to become blind, and a sensible one to turn an ideot. The first of which is unnatural, and the other impossible.

As to the remark, which the Abbe makes, of the one country being a monarchy, and the other a republic, it can have no essential meaning. Forms of Government have nothing to do with treaties. The former are the internal police of the countries, severally; the latter, their external police jointly: and so long as each performs its part, we have no more right, or business, to know how the one or the other conducts its domestic affairs, than we have to enquire into the private concerns of a family.

But had the Abbe reflected for a moment, he would have seen, that Courts, or the governing powers of all countries, be their forms what they may, are, relatively, republics with each other. It is the first, and true principle of alliancing. Antiquity may have given precedence, and power will naturally create importance, but their equal right is never disputed. It may likewise be worthy of remarking, that a monarchical country can suffer nothing in its popular happiness, by allying with a republican one; and republican Governments have never been destroyed by their external connexions, but by some internal convulsion or contrivance; France has been in alliance with the republic of Swisserland, for more than two hundred years, and still Swisserland retains her original form, as entire as if she had allied with a republic like herself; therefore, this remark of the Abbe goes to nothing.—Besides, it is best that mankind should mix. There is ever something to learn, either of manners, or principle; and it is by a free communication, without regard to domestic matters, that friendship is to be extended, and prejudice destroyed all over the world.

But, notwithstanding the Abbe's high professions in favour of liberty, he appears sometimes to forget himself, or that his theory is rather the child of his fancy, than of his judgment; for, in almost the same instant that he censures the alliance as not originally, or sufficiently calculated for the happiness of mankind, he, by a figure of implication, accuses France for having acted so generously and unreservedly in concluding it. "Why did they," says die, meaning the Court of France, "tie themselves down by an inconsiderate treaty to conditions with the Congress, which they might themselves have held in dependence, by ample and regular supplies."

When an author undertakes to treat of public happiness, he ought to be certain that he does not mistake passion for right, nor imagination for principle. Principle, like truth, needs no contrivance. It will ever tell its own tale, and tell it the same way. But where this is not the case, every page must be watched, recollected, and compared, like an invented story.

I am surprised at this passage of the Abbe. It means nothing; or, it means ill; and, in any case, it shews the great difference between speculative and practical knowledge. A treaty, according to the Abbe's language, would have neither duration, nor affection; it might have lasted to the end of the war, and then expired with it.—But France, by acting in a style superior to the little politics of narrow thinking, has established a generous fame, and with the love of a country she was before a stranger to. She had to treat with a People who thought as nature taught them; and, on her own part, she wisely saw there was no present advantage to be obtained by unequal terms, which could balance the more lasting ones that might flow from a kind and generous beginning.

From this part the Abbe advances into the secret transactions of the two Cabinets of Versailles and Madrid, respecting the independence of America; through which I mean not to follow him. It is a circumstance sufficiently striking, without being commented on, that the former union of America with Britain produced a power, which, in her hands, was becoming dangerous, to the world: and there is no improbability in supposing, that, had the latter known as much of the strength of the former before she began the quarrel, as she has known since, that instead of attempting to reduce her to unconditional submission, she would have proposed to her the conquest of Mexico. But from the countries separately, Spain has nothing to apprehend, though from their union she had more to fear than any other power in Europe.

The part which I shall more particularly confine myself to, is that wherein the Abbe takes an opportunity of complimenting the British Ministry with high encomiums of admiration, on their rejecting the offered mediation of the Court of Madrid, in 1779.

It must be remembered, that before Spain joined France in the war, she undertook the office of a Mediator, and made proposals to the British King and Ministry so exceedingly favourable to their interest, that had they been accepted, would have become inconvenient, if not inadmissible, to America. These proposals were nevertheless rejected by the British Cabinet: on which the Abbe says,—

"It is in such a circumstance as this; it is in the time when noble pride elevates the soul superior to all terror; when nothing is seen more dreadful than the shame of receiving the law, and when there is no doubt or hesitation which to chuse between ruin and dishonour; it is then, that the greatness of a Nation is displayed. I acknowledge, however, that men accustomed to judge of things by the event, call great and perilous resolutions, heroism or madness, according to the good or bad success with which they have been attended. If then I should be asked, what is the name which shall in years to come, be given to the firmness which was in this moment exhibited by the English, I shall answer, that I do not know. But that which it deserves I know. I know that the annals of the world hold out to us but rarely the august and majestic spectacle of a Nation, which chuses rather to renounce its duration than its glory."

In this paragraph the conception is lofty, and the expression elegant; but the colouring is too high for the original, and the likeness fails through an excess of graces. To fit the powers of thinking and the turn of language to the subject, so as to bring out a clear conclusion that shall hit the point in question, and nothing else, is the true criterion of writing. But the greater part of the Abbe's writings (if he will pardon me the remark) appear to me uncentral, and burthened with variety. They represent a beautiful wilderness without paths; in which the eye is diverted by every thing, without being particularly directed to any thing: and in which it is agreeable to be lost, and difficult to find the way out.

Before I offer any other remark on the spirit and composition of the above passage, I shall compare it with the circumstance it alludes to.

The circumstance, then, does not deserve the encomium. The rejection was not prompted by her fortitude, but her vanity. She did not view it as a case of despair, or even of extreme danger, and consequently the determination to renounce her duration rather than her glory, cannot apply to the condition of her mind. She had then high expectations of subjugating America, and had no other naval force against her than France; neither was she certain that rejecting the mediation of Spain would combine that power with France. New mediations might arise more favourable than those she had refused. But if they should not, and Spain should join, she still saw that it would only bring out her naval force against France and Spain,

Which was not wanted, and could not be employed against America; and habits of thinking had taught her to believe herself superior to both.

But in any case to which the consequence might point, there was nothing to impress her with the idea of renouncing her duration. It is not the policy of Europe to suffer the extinction of any power, but only to lop off, or prevent its dangerous encrease. She was likewise freed by situation from the internal and immediate horrors of invasion; was rolling in dissipation, and looking for conquests; and though she suffered nothing but the expence of war, she still had a greedy eye to magnificent reimbursement.

But if the Abbe is delighted with high and striking singularities of character, he might, in America, have found ample field for encomium. Here was a people who could not know what part the world would take for, or against them; and who were venturing on an untried scheme, in opposition to a power, against which more formidable Nations had failed. They had every thing to learn but the principles which supported them, and every thing to procure that was necessary for their defence. They have at times seen themselves as low as distress could make them, without shewing the least stagger in their fortitude; and been raised again by the most unexpected events, without discovering an unmanly discomposure of joy. To hesitate or to despair, are conditions equally unknown in America. Her mind was prepared for every thing; because her original and final resolution of succeeding or perishing, included all possible circumstances.

The rejection of the British propositions in the year 1778, circumstanced as America was at that time, is a far greater instance of unshaken fortitude than the refusal of the Spanish mediation by the Court of London: and other historians besides the Abbe, struck with the vastness of her conduct therein, have, like himself, attributed it to a circumstance which was then unknown, the alliance with France. Their error shews the idea of its greatness; because, in order to account for it, they have sought a cause suited to its magnitude, without knowing that the cause existed in the principles of the country.[3]

"The Commissioners, who, in consequence of Lord North's conciliator bills,

---

3 Extract from, " *A short review of the present reign,* " in England. *Page 45, in the New Annual Register for the year* 1780.

went over to America, to propose terms of peace to the colonies were wholly unsuccessful. The concessions which formerly would have been received with the utmost gratitude, were rejected with disdain. Now was the time of American pride and haughtiness. It is probable, however, that it was not pride and haughtiness alone that dictated the Resolutions of Congress, but a distrust of the sincerity of the offers of Britain, a determination not to give up their independence, and ABOVE ALL THE ENGAGEMENTS INTO WHICH THEY HAD ENTERED BY THEIR LATE TREATY WITH FRANCE."]

But this passionate encomium of the Abbe is deservedly subject to moral and philosophical objections. It is the effusion of wild thinking, and has a tendency to prevent that humanity of reflection which the criminal conduct of Britain enjoins on her as a duty.—It is a laudanum to courtly iniquity.—It keeps in intoxicated sleep the conscience of the Nation; and more mischief is affected by wrapping up guilt in splendid excuse, than by directly patronizing it.

Britain is now the only country which holds the world in disturbance and war; and instead of paying compliments to the excess of her crimes, the Abbe would have appeared much more in character, had he put to her, or to her monarch, this serious question—

Are there not miseries enough in the world, too difficult to be encountered, and too pointed to be borne, without studying to enlarge the list, and arming it with new destruction? Is life so very long, that it is necessary, nay even a duty, to shake the sand, and hasten out the period of duration? Is the path so elegantly smooth, so decked on every side, and carpeted with joys, that wretchedness is wanted to enrich it as a soil? Go, ask thine aching heart, when sorrow from a thousand causes wound it; go, ask thy sickened self, when every medicine fails, whether this be the case or not?

Quitting my remarks on this head, I proceed to another, in which the Abbe has let loose a vein of ill-nature, and what is still worse, of injustice.

After cavilling at the treaty, he goes on to characterize the several parties combined in the war.—"Is it possible," says the Abbe, "that a strict union should long subsist amongst confederates of characters so opposite as the hasty, light, disdainful Frenchman, the jealous, haughty, sly, slow, circumspective Spaniard; and the American, who is secretly snatching looks at the mother country, and would rejoice, were they compatible with his independence, at the disasters of his allies?"

To draw foolish portraits of each other, is a mode of attack and reprisal, which the greater part of mankind are fond of indulging. The serious philosopher should be above it, more especially in cases from which no possible good can arise, and mischief may, and where no received provocation can palliate the offence.—The Abbe might have invented a difference of character for every country in the world, and they in return might find others for him, till in the war of wit all real character is lost. The pleasantry of one Nation or the gravity of another may, by a little penciling, be distorted into whimsical features, and the painter become as much laughed at as the painting.

But why did not the Abbe look a little deeper, and bring forth the excellencies of the several parties? Why did he not dwell with pleasure on that greatness of character, that superiority of heart, which has marked the conduct of France in her conquests, and which has forced an acknowledgment even from Britain?

There is one line, at least (and many others might be discovered) in which the confederates unite, which is, that of a rival eminence in their treatment of their enemies. Spain, in her conquest of Minorca and the Bahama Islands, confirms this remark. America has been invariable in her lenity from the beginning of the war, notwithstanding the high provocations she has experienced. It is England only who has been insolent and cruel.

But why must America be charged with a crime undeserved by her conduct, more so by her principles, and which, if a fact would be fatal to her honour? I mean that of want of attachment to her allies, or rejoicing in their disasters. She, it is true, has been assiduous in shewing to the world that she was not the aggressor towards England; that the quarrel was not of her seeking, or, at that time, even of her wishing. But to draw inferences from her candour, and even from her justification, to stab her character by, and I see nothing else from which they can be supposed to be drawn, is unkind and unjust.

Does her rejection of the British propositions in 1778, before she knew of any alliance with France, correspond with the Abbe's description of her mind? Does a single instance of her conduct since that time justify it?—But there it a still better evidence to apply to, which is, that of all the mails which at different times have been way laid on the road, in divers parts of America, and taken and carried into

New York, and from which the most secret and confidental private letters, as well as those from authority, have been published, not one of them, I repeat it, not a single one of them, gives countenance to such a charge.

This is not a country where men are under Government restraint in speaking; and if there is any kind of restraint, it arises from a fear of popular resentment. Now, if nothing in her private or public correspondence favours such a suggestion, and if the general disposition of the country is such as to make it unsafe for a man to shew an appearance of joy at any disaster to her ally, on what grounds, I ask, can the accusation stand? What company the Abbe may have kept in France, we cannot know; but this we know, that the account he gives does not apply to America.

Had the Abbe been in America at the time the news arrived of the disaster of the fleet under Count de Grasse, in the West Indies, he would have seen his vast mistake. Neither do I remember any instance, except the loss of Charlestown, in which the public mind suffered more severe and pungent concern, or underwent more agitations of hope and apprehension, as to the truth or falsehood of the report. Had the loss been all our own, it could not have had a deeper effect, yet it was not one of these cases which reached to the independence of America.

In the geographical account which the Abbe gives of the Thirteen States, he is so exceedingly erroneous, that to attempt a particular refutation, would exceed the limits I have prescribed to myself. And as it is a matter neither political, historical, nor sentimental, and which can always be contradicted by the extent and natural circumstances of the country, I shall pass it over; with this additional remark, that I never yet saw an European description of America that was true, neither can any person gain a just idea of it, but by coming to it.

Though I have already extended this letter beyond what I at first proposed, I am, nevertheless, obliged to omit many observations, I originally designed to have made. I wish there had been no occasion for making any. But the wrong ideas which the Abbe's work had a tendency to excite, and the prejudicial impressions they might make, must be an apology for my remarks, and the freedom with which they are done.

I observe the Abbe has made a sort of epitome of a considerable part of the pamphlet COMMON SENSE, and introduced it in that form into his publication. But there are other places where the Abbe has borrowed freely from the same pamphlet, without acknowledging it. The difference between Society and Government, with which the pamphlet opens, is taken from it, and in some expressions almost literally, into the Abbe's work, as if originally his own; and through the whole of the Abbe's remarks on this head, the idea in Common Sense is so closely copied and pursued, that the difference is only in words, and in the arrangement of the thoughts, and not in the thoughts themselves[4]

COMMON SENSE.

"Some writers have so confounded society with Government, as to leave little or no distinction between them; whereas they are not only different, but have different origins.

"Society is produced by our wants, and Government by our wickedness; the former promotes our happiness positively, by uniting our affections; the latter negatively, by restraining our vices."

"In order to gain a clear and just idea of the design and end of Government, let us suppose a small number of persons meeting in some sequestered part of the earth unconnected with the rest; they will then represent the peopling of any country or of the world. In this state of natural liberty, society will be their first thought. A thousand motives will excite them thereto. The strength of one man is so unequal to his wants, and his mind so unfitted for perpetual solitude, that he is soon obliged to seek assistance of another, who, in his turn, requires the same. Four or five united would be able to raise a tolerable dwelling in the midst of a wilderness; but one man might labour out the common period of life, without accomplishing any thing: when he had felled his timber he could not remove it, nor erect it after it was removed; hunger, in the mean time, would urge him from his work, and every different want call him a different way. Disease, nay even misfortune, would be death; for though neither might be immediately mortal, yet either of them would disable him from living and reduce him to a state in which he might rather be

---

4 *In the following paragraph there is less likeness in the language, but the ideas in the one are evidently copied from the other.*

said to perish than to die.—Thus necessity, like a gravitating power, would form our newly arrived emigrants into society, the reciprocal blessings of which would supersede and render the obligations of law and Government unnecessary, while they remained perfectly just to each other. But as nothing but Heaven is impregnable to vice, it will unavoidably happen, that in proportion as they surmount the first difficulties of emigration which bound them together in a common cause, they will begin to relax in their duty and attachment to each other, and this remissness will point out the necessity of establishing some form of Government to supply the defect of moral virtue."

ABBE RAYNAL.

"Care must be taken not to confound together society with Government. That they may be known distinctly, their origin should be considered.

"Society originates in the their vices. Society tends always to good; Government ought always to tend to the repressing of evil."

Man, thrown as it were by chance upon the globe, surrounded by all the evils of nature, obliged continually to defend and protect his life against the storms and tempests of the air, against the inundations of water, against the fire of volcanoes, against the intemperance of frigid and torrid zones, against the sterility of the earth, which refuses him, aliment, or its baneful secundity, which makes poison spring up beneath his feet; in short, against the claws and teeth of savage beasts, who dispute with him his habitation and his prey, and attacking his person, seem, resolved to render themselves rulers of this globe, of which he thigks himself to be the master. Man, in this state, alone and abandoned to himself, could do nothing for his preservation. It was necessary, therefore, that he should unite himself, and associate with his like, in order to bring together their strength and intelligence in common stock. It is by this union that he has triumphed over so many evils, that he has fashioned this globe to his use, restrained the livers, subjugated the seas, insured his subsistence, conquered a part of the animals in obliging them to serve him, and driven others far from his empire to the depth of deserts or of woods, where their number diminishes from age to age. What a man alone would not have been able to effect, men have executed in concert; and altogether they preserve their work.—Such is the origin, such the advantages, and the end of society.—Government owes its birth to the necessity of preventing and repressing the injuries which the associated individuals had to fear from one another. It is the centinel who watches, in order that the common labours be not disturbed."].

But as it is time I should come to a conclusion of my letter, I shall forbear all further observations on the Abbe's work, and take a concise view of the state of public affairs, since the time in which that performance was published.

A mind habited to actions of meanness and injustice, commits them without reflection, or with a very partial one; for on what other ground than this, can we account for the declaration of war against the Dutch? To gain an idea of the politics which actuated the British Ministry to this measure, we must enter into the opinion which they, and the English in general, had formed of the temper of the Dutch Nation; and from thence infer what their expectation of the consequence would be.

Could they have imagined that Holland would have seriously made a common cause with France, Spain, and America, the British Ministry would never have dared to provoke them. It would have been a madness in politics to have done so; unless their views were to hasten on a period of such emphatic distress, as should justify the concessions which they saw they must one day or other make to the world, and for which they wanted an apology to themselves.—There is a temper in some men which seeks a pretence for submission. Like a ship disabled in action, and unfitted to continue it, it waits the approach of a still larger one to strike to, and feels relief at the opportunity. Whether this is greatness or littleness of mind, I am not enquiring into. I should suppose it to be the latter, because it proceeds from the want of knowing how to bear misfortune in its original state.

But the consequent conduct of the British cabinet has shewn that this was not their plan of politics, and consequently their motives must be sought for in another line.

The truth is, that the British had formed a very humble opinion of the Dutch Nation. They looked on them as a People who would submit to any thing; that they might insult them as they liked, plunder them as they pleased, and still the Dutch dared not to be provoked.

If this be taken as the opinion of the British cabinet, the measure is easily accounted for, because it goes on the supposition, that when, by a declaration of hostilities, they had robbed the Dutch of some millions sterling, (and to rob then was popular) they could make peace with them again whenever they pleased, and on almost any terms the British Ministry should propose. And no sooner was the plundering committed, than the accommodation was set on foot, and failed.

When once the mind loses the sense of its own dignity, it loses, likewise, the ability of judging of it in another. And the American war has thrown Britain into such a variety of absurd situations, that arguing from herself, she sees not in what conduct National dignity consists in other countries: From Holland she expected duplicity and submission, and this mistake arose from her having acted, in a number of instances during the present war, the same character herself.

To be allied to, or connected with Britain, seems to be an unsafe and impolitic situation. Holland and America are instances of the reality of this remark. Make those countries the allies of France or Spain, and Britain will court them with civility, and treat them with respect; make them her own allies, and she will insult and plunder them. In the first case, she feels some apprehensions at offending them, because they have support at hand; in the latter, those apprehensions do not exist. Such, however, has hitherto been her conduct.

Another measure which has taken place since the publication of the Abbe's work, and likewise since the time of my beginning this letter, is the change in the British Ministry. What line the new cabinet will pursue respecting America, is at this time unknown; neither is it very material, unless they are seriously disposed to a general and honourable peace.

Repeated experience has shewn, not only the impracticability of conquering America, but the still higher impossibility of conquering her mind, or recalling her back to her former condition of thinking. Since the commencement of the war, which is now approaching, to eight years, thousands, and tens of thousands, have advanced, and are daily advancing into the first state of manhood, who know nothing of Britain but as a barbarous enemy, and to whom the independence of America appears as much the natural and established Government of the country, as that of England does to an Englishman. And on the other hand, thousands of the aged, who had British ideas, have dropped, and are daily dropping, from the stage of business and life.—The natural progress of generation and decay, operates every hour to the disadvantage of Britain. Time and death, hard enemies to contend with, fight-constantly against her interest; and the bills of mortality, in every part of America, are the thermometers of her decline. The children in the streets are, from their cradle, bred to consider her as their only foe. They hear of her cruelties; of their-fathers, uncles, and kindred killed; they see the remains of burnt and destroyed houses, and the common tradition of the school they go to, tells them, ***those things were done by the British.***

These are circumstances which the mere English state-politician, who considers man only in a state of manhood, does not attend to. He gets entangled with parties coeval or equal with himself at home, and thinks not how fast the rising generation in America is growing beyond his knowledge of them, or they of him. In a few years, all personal remembrance will be lost, and who is King or Minister in England, will be little known, and scarcely enquired after.

The new British Administration is composed of persons who have ever been against the war, and who have constantly reprobated all the violent measures of the former one. They considered the American war as destructive to themselves, and opposed it on that ground. But what are these things to America? She has nothing to do with English parties. The Ins and the Outs are nothing to her. It is the whole country she is at war with, or must be at peace with.

Were every Minister in England a ***Chatham,*** it would now weigh little or nothing in the scale of American politics. Death has preserved to the memory of this Statesman, ***that fame,*** which he, by living, would have lost. His plans and opinions, towards the latter part of his life, would have been attended with as many evil consequences, and as much reprobated here, as those of Lord North; and considering him a wise man, they abound with inconsistencies amounting to absurdities.

It has, apparently, been the fault of many in the late-Minority, to suppose, that America would agree to certain terms with them, were they in place, which she would not ever listen to from the then Administration. This idea can answer no other purpose than to prolong the war; and Britain may, at the expence of many more millions, learn the fatality of such mistakes. If the new Ministry wisely avoid this hopeless policy, they will prove themselves better pilots, and wiser men than they are conceived to be; for it is every day expected to see their bark strike upon some hidden rock and go to pieces.

But there is a line in which they may be great. A more brilliant opening needs not to present itself; and it is such an one, as true magnanimity would improve, and humanity rejoice in.

A total reformation is wanted in England. She wants an expanded mind,—an heart which embraces the universe. Instead of shutting herself up in an island, and quarrelling with the world, she would derive more lasting happiness, and acquire more real riches, by generously mixing with it, and bravely saying, I am the enemy of none. It is not now a time for little contrivances, or artful politics. The European world is too experienced to be imposed upon, and America too wise to be duped. It must be something new and masterly that must succeed. The idea of seducing America from her independence, or corrupting her from her alliance, is a thought too little for a great mind, and impossible for any honest one to attempt. Whenever politics are applied to debauch mankind from their integrity, and dissolve the virtues of human nature, they become detestable, and to be a stateman upon this plan, is to be a commissioned villain. He who aims at it, leaves a vacancy in his character, which may be filled up with the worst of epithets.

If the disposition of England should be such, as not to agree to a general and honourable peace, and that the war must, at all events, continue longer, I cannot help wishing that the alliances which America has or may enter into, may become the only objects of the war. She wants an opportunity of shewing to the world, that she holds her honour as dear and sacred as her independence, and that she will, in no situation, forsake those, whom no negociations could induce to forsake her. Peace to every reflective mind is a desirable object; but that peace which is accompanied with a ruined character, becomes a crime to the seducer, and a curse upon the seduced.

But where is the impossibility, or even the great difficulty, of England forming a friendship with France and Spain, and making it a National virtue to renounce for ever those prejudiced inveteracies it has been her custom to cherish; and which, while they serve to sink her with an increasing enormity of debt, by involving her in fruitless wars, become likewise, the bane of her repose, and the destruction of her manners. We had once the fetters that she has now, but experience has shewn us the mistake, and thinking justly has set us right.

The true idea of a great Nation, is, that which extends and promotes the principles of universal society; whose mind rises above the atmosphere of local thoughts, and considers mankind, of whatever nation or profession they may be, as the work, of one Creator. The rage for conquest has had its fashion and its day. Why may not the amiable virtues have the same? The Alexanders and Caesars of antiquity, have left behind them their monuments of destruction, and are remembered with hatred; while these more exalted characters, who first taught society and science, are blessed with the gratitude of every age and country. Of more use was one philosopher though a heathen, to the world, than all the heathen conquerors that ever existed.

Should the present revolution be distinguished by opening a new system of extended civilization, it will receive from heaven the highest evidence of approbation; and as this is a subject to which the Abbe's power are so eminently suited, I recommend it to his attention, with the affection of a friend, and the ardour of an universal citizen.

POSTSCRIPT.

SINCE closing the foregoing letter, some intimations respecting a general peace, have, made their way to America. On what authority or foundation they stand, or how near, or how remote such an event may be, are circumstances, I am not enquiring into. But as the subject must, sooner or later, become a matter of serious attention, it may not be improper, even at this early period, candidly to investigate some points that are connected with it, or lead towards it.

The independence of America is at this moment, as firmly established as that of any other country in a state of war. It is not length of time, but power, that gives stability. Nations at war, know nothing of each other on the score of antiquity. It is their present and immediate strength, together with their connections, that must support them. To which we may add, that a right which originated to-day, is as much aright, as if it had the sanction of a thousand years and, therefore, the independence and present Government of America are in no more danger of being subverted, because they are modern, than that of England is secure, because it is ancient.

The politics of Britain, so far as they respected America, were originally conceived in idiotism, and acted in madness. There is not a step which bears the smallest trace of rationality. In her management of the war, she has laboured be wretched, and studied to be hated; and in all her former propositions for accommodation, she has discovered a total, ignorance of mankind, and of those natural and unalterable sensations by which they are so generally governed. How-she may conduct herself in the present or future business of negotiating a peace is yet to be proved.

He is a weak politician who does not understand human nature, and penetrate into the effect which measures of Government will have upon the mind. All the miscarriages of Britain have arisen from this defect. The former Ministry acted as if they supposed mankind to be *without a mind;* and the present Ministry, as if America was *without a memory.* The one must have supposed we were incapable of feeling; and the other that we could not remember injuries.

There is likewise another line in which politicians mistake, which is that of not rightly calculating, to rather of misjudging, the consequence which any given circumstance will produce. Nothing is more frequent, as well in common as in political life, than to hear people complain, that such and such means produced an event directly contrary to their intentions. But the fault lies in their not judging rightly what the event would be; for the means produced only their proper and natural consequences.

It is very probable, that in a treaty of peace, Britain will contend for some post or other in North America; perhaps Canada or Halifax, or both: and I infer this from the known deficiency of her politics, which have ever yet made use of means, whose natural event was against both her interest and her expectation. But the question with her ought to be, Whether it is worth her while to hold them, and what will be the consequence?

Respecting Canada, one or other of the two following will take place, viz. If Canada should people, it will revolt, and of it do not people, it will not be worth the expence of holding. And the same may be said of Halifax, and the country round it. But Canada *never will* people; neither is there any occasion for contrivances on one side or the other, for nature alone will do the whole.

Britain may put herself to great expences in sending settlers to Canada; but the descendants of those settlers will be Americans, as other descendants have been before them. They will look round and see the neighbouring States sovereign and free, respected abroad, and trading at large with the world; and the natural love of liberty, the advantages of commerce, the blessings of independence, and of a happier climate, and a richer soil, will draw them southward, and the effect will be, that Britain will sustain the expence, and America reap the advantage.

One would think that the experience which Britain has lad of America, would entirely sicken her of all thoughts of continental colonization; and any part which she might retain, would only become to her a field of jealousy and thorns, of debate and contention, for ever struggling for privileges, and meditating revolt. She may form new settlements, but they will be for us; they will become part of the United States of America; and that against all her contrivances to prevent it, or without any endeavours of ours to promote it. In the first place, she cannot draw from them a revenue until they are able to pay one, and when they are so, they will be above subjection. Men soon become attached to the soil they live upon, and incorporated with the prosperity of the place; and it signifies but little, what opinions they come over with, for time, interest, and new connections, will render them obsolete, and the next generations know nothing of them.

Were Britain truly wise she would lay hold of the present opportunity, to disentangle herself from all continental embarrassments in North America, and that not only to avoid future broils and troubles, but to save expences. For to speak explicitly on the matter, I would not, were I an European power, have Canada, under the conditions that Britain must retain it, could it be given to me. It is one of those kind of dominions that is, and ever will be, a constant charge upon any foreign holder.

As to Halifax, it will become useless to England after the present war, and the loss of the United States. A harbour, when the dominion is gone, for the purpose of which only it was wanted, can be attended only with expence. There are, I doubt not, thousands of people in England, who suppose, that those places are a profit to the Nation, whereas, they are directly the contrary, and instead of producing any revenue, a considerable part of the revenue of England is annually drawn off, to support the expence of holding them.

Gibraltar is another instance of National ill-policy. A post which, in time of peace, is not wanted, and in time of war, is of no use, must, at all times, be useless. Instead of affording protection to a Navy, it requires the aid of one to maintain it. And to suppose that Gibraltar commands the Mediterranean, or the pass into it, or the trade of it, is to suppose a detected falsehood; because, though Britain holds the post, she has lost the other three, and every benefit she expected from it. And to say that all this happens because it is besieged by land and water, is to say nothing, for this will always be the case in time of war, while France and Spain keep up superior fleets, and Britain holds the place—So that, though as an impenetrable, inaccessible rock, it may be held by the one, it is always in the power of the other to render it useless, and excessively chargeable.

I should suppose that one of the principal objects of Spain in besieging it, is to shew to Britain, that though she may not take it, she can cammand it, that is, she can shut it up, and prevent its being used as a harbour, though not as a garrison.— But the short way to reduce Gibraltar is to at tack the British fleet; for Gibraltar is as dependent on a fleet for support, as a bird is on its wings for food, and when wounded there, it starves.

There is another circumstance which the people of England have not only not attended to, but seem to be utterly ignorant of, and that is, the difference between permanent power, and accidental power, considered in a National sense.

By permanent power, I mean, a natural, inherent, and perpetual ability in a Nation, which, though always in being, may not be always in action, or not always advantageously directed; and by accidental power, I mean, a fortunate or accidental disposition or exercise of National strength, in whole or in part.

There undoubtedly was a time when any one European Nation, with only eight or ten ships of war, equal to the present ships of the line, could have carried terror to all others, who had not began to build a navy, however great their natural ability might be for that purpose. But this can be considered only as accidental, and not as a standard to compare permanent power by, and could last no longer than until those powers built as many or more ships than the former. After this, a larger fleet was necessary, in order to-be superior; and a still larger would again supersede it. And thus mankind have gone on, building fleet upon fleet, as occasion or situation dictated. And this reduces it to an original question, which is,—Which power can build and man the largest number of ships? The natural answer to which, is, That power which has the largest revenue, and the greatest number of inhabitants, provided its situation of coast affords sufficient conveniencies.

France being a Nation on the continent of Europe, and Britain an island in its neighbourhood, each of them derived different ideas from their different situations. The inhabitants of Britain could carry on no foreign trade, nor stir from the spot they dwelt upon, without the assistance of shipping; but this was not the case with France. The idea, therefore, of a navy did not arise to France from the same original and immediate necessity which produced it to England. But the question is, that when both of them turn their attention, and employ their revenues the same way, which can be superior?

The annual revenue of France is nearly double that of England, and her number of inhabitants more than twice as many. Each of them has the same length of coast on the channel; besides which, France has several hundred miles extent on the Bay of Biscay, and an opening on the Mediterranean: and every day proves, that practice and exercise make sailors, as well as soldiers, in one country as well as another.

If, then, Britain can maintain an hundred ships of the line, France can as well support an hundred and fifty, because her revenues, and her population, are as equal to the one, as those of England are to the other. And the only reason why she has not done it, is, because she has not, till very lately, attended to it. But when she sees, as she now sees, that a navy is the first engine of power, she can easily accomplish it.

England very falsely, and ruinously for herself, infers, that because she had the advantage of France, while France had a smaller navy, that for that reason it is always to be so. Whereas, it may be clearly seen, that the strength of France has never yet been tried on a navy, and that she is able to be as superior to England in the extent of a navy, as she is in the extent of her revenues and her population. And England may lament the day when, by her insolence and injustice, she provoked in France a maritime disposition.

It is in the power of the combined fleets to conquer every island in the West Indies, and reduce all the British navy in those places. For were France and Spain to send their whole naval force in Europe to those islands, it would not be in the power of Britain to follow them with an equal force. She would still be twenty or thirty ships inferior, were she to send every vessel she had; and, in the mean time, all the foreign trade of England would lay exposed to the Dutch.

It is a maxim which, I am persuaded, will ever hold good, and more especially in naval operations, that a great power ought never to move in detachments, if it can possibly be avoided; but to go with its whole force to some important object, the reduction of which shall have a decisive effect upon the war. Had the whole of the French and Spanish fleets in Europe come last spring to the West Indies, every island had been their own, Rodney their prisoner, and his fleet their prize. From the United States, the combined fleets can be supplied with provisions, without the necessity of drawing them from Europe, which is not the case with England.

Accident as thrown some advantages in the way of England, which, from the inferiority of her navy, she had not a right to expect. For though she has been obliged to fly before the combined fleets, yet Rodney has twice had the fortune to fall in with detached squadrons, to which he was superior in numbers. The first off Cape St. Vincent, where he had nearly two to one; and the other in the West Indies, where he had a majority of six ships. Victories of this kind almost produce themselves. They are won without, honour, and suffered without disgrace; and are ascribable to the chance of meeting, not to the superiority of fighting. For the same Admiral, under whom they were obtained, was unable, in three former engagements, to make the least impression on a fleet consisting of an equal number of ships with his own, and compounded for the events by declining the actions[5].

To conclude, if it may be said, that Britain has numerous enemies, it likewise proves that she has given numerous offences. Insolence is sure to provoke hatred, whether in a Nation or an individual. The want of manners in the British Court, may be seen even in its birth-day and new-, year's odes, which are calculated to infatuate the vulgar, and disgust the man of refinement; and her former overbearing, rudeness, and insufferable injustice on the seas, have made every commercial Nation her foe. Her fleets were employed as engines of prey; and acted on the surface of the deep, the character which the shark does beneath it.—On the other hand, the Combined Powers are taking a popular part,, and will render their reputation immortal, by establishing, the perfect freedom of the ocean, to which all countries have a right, and are interested in accomplishing. The sea is the world's highway;

---

5 See the accounts, either English or French, of the actions in the West-Indies between Count de Guichen, and Admiral Rodneys, in 1780.

and he who arrogates a prerogative over it, transgresses the right, and justly brings on himself the chastisement of Nations.

Perhaps it might be of some service to the future tranquillity of mankind, were an article introduced into the next general peace, that no one Nation should, in time of peace, exceed a certain number of ships of war. Something of this kind seems necessary; for, according to the present fashion, half the world will get upon the water, and there appears to be no end to the extent to which navies may be carried. Another reason is, that navies add nothing to the manners or morals of a people. The sequestered life which attends the service, prevents the opportunities of society, and is too apt to occasion a coarseness of ideas and of language, and that more in ships of war than in commercial employ; because, in the latter, they mix more with the world, and are nearer related to it. I mention this remark as a general one, and not applied to any one country more than to another.

Britain has now had the trial of above seven years, with an expence of nearly a hundred million pounds sterling; and every month in which she delays to conclude a peace, costs her another million sterling, over and above her ordinary expences of Government, which are a million more; so that her total *monthly* expence is two million pounds sterling, which is equal to the whole *yearly* expence of America, all charges included. Judge then who is best able to continue it.

She has, likewise, many atonements to make to an injured world, as well in one quarter as another. And instead of pursuing that temper of arrogance, which serves only to sink her in the esteem, and entail on her the dislike, of all Nations, she will do well to reform her manners, retrench her expences, live peaceably with her neighbours, and think of war no more.

Philadelphia, August 21, 1782.

THE END.

APPENDIX.

As the following correspondence relates to the LETTER To.
THE ABBE RAYNAL it is deemed proper to introduce, it here; for though pri-

vate letters are entitled to secrecy and confidence, yet when they relate to matters in which every body is interested, and no possible inconvenience can arise from the publication of them, they may afford not only amusement, but advantage. The late revolution has, doubtless, produced many letters of this, kind, which, at some future period, would be esteemed both curious and useful. The two following letters have nothing very material in them, otherwise than the latter of them shews, that the writer of it, notwithstanding all the difficulties and severities he experienced at the head of the army, was to the last devoted to undergo a further continuance of them, or any new hardships that might arise.

Borden Town, Sep. 7, 1782.

SIR,

I have the honour of presenting you with fifty copies of my letter to the Abbe Raynal, for the use of the army, and to repeat to you my acknowledgments for your friendship.

I fully believe we have seen our worst days over.—The spirit of the war, on the part of the enemy, is certainly on the decline, full as much as we think for. I draw his opinion not only from the present promising appearance of things, and the difficulties we know the British cabinet is in; but I add to it the peculiar effect which certain periods of time, have more or less, upon all men.

The British have accustomed themselves to think of seven years in a manner different to other portions of lime. They acquire this partly by habit, by reason, by religion, and by superstition. They serve seven years apprenticeship—they elect their parliament for seven years—they punish by seven years transportation, or the duplicate or triplicate of that term—they let their leases in the same manner, and they read that Jacob served seven years for one wife, and after that seven years for another; and this particular period of time, by a variety of concurrences, has obtained an influence in their mind.

They have now had seven years of war, and are no further on the continent than when they began. The superstitious and populous part will therefore conclude that it is not to be, and the rational part of them will think they have tried an unsuccessful and expensive project long enough, so that by these two joining issue in the same eventual opinion, the obstinate part among them will be beaten out; unless, consistent with their former sagacity, they should get over the matter by an act of parliament, "to bind time in all cases whatsoever," or declare him a rebel.

I observe the affair of Captain Asgill seems to die away:—very probably it has been protracted on the part of Clinton and Carleton to gain time, to state the case to the British ministry, where following close on that of Colonel Haynes, it will create new embarrassments to them.—For my own part, I am fully persuaded that a suspension of his fate, still holding it *in terrorem,* will operate on a greater quantity of their passions and vices, and restrain them more than his execution would do.—However the change of measures which seems now to be taking place, gives somewhat of a new cast to former designs; and if the case, without the execution, can be so managed as to answer all the purposes of the latter, it will look much better hereafter, when the sensations that now provoke, and the circumstances that would justify his exit, shall be forgotten.

I am your Excellency's obliged and obedient humble servant, THOMAS PAINE.

His Excellency General Washington.
Head-Quarters, Verplank's Point. Sep. 18, 1782.

SIR,

I have the pleasure to acknowledge your favor of the 7th inst. informing me of your proposal to present me with fifty copies of your last publication, for the amusement of the army.

For this intention you have my sincere thanks, not only on my own account, but for the pleasure, I doubt not, the gentlemen of the army will receive from the perusal of your pamphlets.

Your observations on the period of seven years, as it applies itself to, and affects British minds, are ingenious, and I wish it may not fail of its effects in the present instance.—The measures, and the policy of the enemy are at present, in great perplexity and embarrassment—but I have my fears, whether their necessities (which are the only operative motive with them) are yet arrived to that point, which must drive them unavoidably into what they will esteem disagreeable and dishonourable terms of peace—such for instance as an absolute, unequivocal admission of American Independence, upon which she can alone accept it.

For this reason, added to the principles of some of the English ministers, I have not so full a confidence in the success of the present negociation for peace as some gentlemen entertain.

Should events prove my jealousies to be ill founded, I shall make myself happy under the mistake—consoling myself with the idea of having erred on the safest side and enjoying with as much satisfaction as any of my countrymen, the pleasing issue of our severe contest.

The case of Capt. Asgill has indeed been spun out to a great length—but with you, I hope, that its termination will not be unfavourable to this country.

I am Sir, with great esteem and regard, Your most obedient servant, G. WASHINGTON,

Thomas Paine, Esquire.

The Codes Of Hammurabi And Moses
W. W. Davies

QTY

The discovery of the Hammurabi Code is one of the greatest achievements of archaeology, and is of paramount interest, not only to the student of the Bible, but also to all those interested in ancient history...

Religion   **ISBN: *1-59462-338-4***   **Pages:132**
MSRP $12.95

The Theory of Moral Sentiments
Adam Smith

QTY

This work from 1749. contains original theories of conscience amd moral judgment and it is the foundation for systemof morals.

Philosophy ISBN: *1-59462-777-0*   **Pages:536**
MSRP $19.95

Jessica's First Prayer
Hesba Stretton

QTY

In a screened and secluded corner of one of the many railway-bridges which span the streets of London there could be seen a few years ago, from five o'clock every morning until half past eight, a tidily set-out coffee-stall, consisting of a trestle and board, upon which stood two large tin cans, with a small fire of charcoal burning under each so as to keep the coffee boiling during the early hours of the morning when the work-people were thronging into the city on their way to their daily toil...

Childrens   ISBN: *1-59462-373-2*   **Pages:84**
MSRP $9.95

My Life and Work
Henry Ford

QTY

Henry Ford revolutionized the world with his implementation of mass production for the Model T automobile. Gain valuable business insight into his life and work with his own auto-biography... "We have only started on our development of our country we have not as yet, with all our talk of wonderful progress, done more than scratch the surface. The progress has been wonderful enough but..."

Biographies/   ISBN: *1-59462-198-5*   **Pages:300**
MSRP $21.95

The Art of Cross-Examination
Francis Wellman

QTY

I presume it is the experience of every author, after his first book is published upon an important subject, to be almost overwhelmed with a wealth of ideas and illustrations which could readily have been included in his book, and which to his own mind, at least, seem to make a second edition inevitable. Such certainly was the case with me; and when the first edition had reached its sixth impression in five months, I rejoiced to learn that it seemed to my publishers that the book had met with a sufficiently favorable reception to justify a second and considerably enlarged edition. ...

Pages:412

Reference   ISBN: *1-59462-647-2*   *MSRP $19.95*

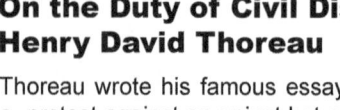

On the Duty of Civil Disobedience
Henry David Thoreau

QTY

Thoreau wrote his famous essay, On the Duty of Civil Disobedience, as a protest against an unjust but popular war and the immoral but popular institution of slave-owning. He did more than write—he declined to pay his taxes, and was hauled off to gaol in consequence. Who can say how much this refusal of his hastened the end of the war and of slavery ?

Law   ISBN: *1-59462-747-9*   **Pages:48**

MSRP $7.45

Dream Psychology
Psychoanalysis for Beginners

Sigmund Freud

Dream Psychology Psychoanalysis for Beginners
Sigmund Freud

QTY

Sigmund Freud, born Sigismund Schlomo Freud (May 6, 1856 - September 23, 1939), was a Jewish-Austrian neurologist and psychiatrist who co-founded the psychoanalytic school of psychology. Freud is best known for his theories of the unconscious mind, especially involving the mechanism of repression; his redefinition of sexual desire as mobile and directed towards a wide variety of objects; and his therapeutic techniques, especially his understanding of transference in the therapeutic relationship and the presumed value of dreams as sources of insight into unconscious desires.

Pages:196

Psychology   ISBN: *1-59462-905-6*   *MSRP $15.45*

The Miracle of Right Thought
Orison Swett Marden

QTY

Believe with all of your heart that you will do what you were made to do. When the mind has once formed the habit of holding cheerful, happy, prosperous pictures, it will not be easy to form the opposite habit. It does not matter how improbable or how far away this realization may see, or how dark the prospects may be, if we visualize them as best we can, as vividly as possible, hold tenaciously to them and vigorously struggle to attain them, they will gradually become actualized, realized in the life. But a desire, a longing without endeavor, a yearning abandoned or held indifferently will vanish without realization.

Pages:360

Self Help   ISBN: *1-59462-644-8*   *MSRP $25.45*

QTY

☐ **The Rosicrucian Cosmo-Conception Mystic Christianity** by *Max Heindel*   ISBN: *1-59462-188-8*   **$38.95**
The Rosicrucian Cosmo-conception is not dogmatic, neither does it appeal to any other authority than the reason of the student. It is: not controversial, but is: sent forth in the, hope that it may help to clear...   New Age/Religion Pages 646

☐ **Abandonment To Divine Providence** by *Jean-Pierre de Caussade*   ISBN: *1-59462-228-0*   **$25.95**
"The Rev. Jean Pierre de Caussade was one of the most remarkable spiritual writers of the Society of Jesus in France in the 18th Century. His death took place at Toulouse in 1751. His works have gone through many editions and have been republished...   Inspirational/Religion Pages 400

☐ **Mental Chemistry** by *Charles Haanel*   ISBN: *1-59462-192-6*   **$23.95**
Mental Chemistry allows the change of material conditions by combining and appropriately utilizing the power of the mind. Much like applied chemistry creates something new and unique out of careful combinations of chemicals the mastery of mental chemistry...   New Age Pages 354

☐ **The Letters of Robert Browning and Elizabeth Barret Barrett 1845-1846 vol II**   ISBN: *1-59462-193-4*   **$35.95**
by *Robert Browning* and *Elizabeth Barrett*   Biographies Pages 596

☐ **Gleanings In Genesis (volume I)** by *Arthur W. Pink*   ISBN: *1-59462-130-6*   **$27.45**
Appropriately has Genesis been termed "the seed plot of the Bible" for in it we have, in germ form, almost all of the great doctrines which are afterwards fully developed in the books of Scripture which follow...   Religion/Inspirational Pages 420

☐ **The Master Key** by *L. W. de Laurence*   ISBN: *1-59462-001-6*   **$30.95**
In no branch of human knowledge has there been a more lively increase of the spirit of research during the past few years than in the study of Psychology, Concentration and Mental Discipline. The requests for authentic lessons in Thought Control, Mental Discipline and...   New Age/Business Pages 422

☐ **The Lesser Key Of Solomon Goetia** by *L. W. de Laurence*   ISBN: *1-59462-092-X*   **$9.95**
This translation of the first book of the "Lernegton" which is now for the first time made accessible to students of Talismanic Magic was done, after careful collation and edition, from numerous Ancient Manuscripts in Hebrew, Latin, and French...   New Age/Occult Pages 92

☐ **Rubaiyat Of Omar Khayyam** by *Edward Fitzgerald*   ISBN:*1-59462-332-5*   **$13.95**
Edward Fitzgerald, whom the world has already learned, in spite of his own efforts to remain within the shadow of anonymity, to look upon as one of the rarest poets of the century, was born at Bredfield, in Suffolk, on the 31st of March, 1809. He was the third son of John Purcell...   Music Pages 172

☐ **Ancient Law** by *Henry Maine*   ISBN: *1-59462-128-4*   **$29.95**
The chief object of the following pages is to indicate some of the earliest ideas of mankind, as they are reflected in Ancient Law, and to point out the relation of those ideas to modern thought.   Religion/History Pages 452

☐ **Far-Away Stories** by *William J. Locke*   ISBN: *1-59462-129-2*   **$19.45**
"Good wine needs no bush, but a collection of mixed vintages does. And this book is just such a collection. Some of the stories I do not want to remain buried for ever in the museum files of dead magazine-numbers an author's not unpardonable vanity..."   Fiction Pages 272

☐ **Life of David Crockett** by *David Crockett*   ISBN: *1-59462-250-7*   **$27.45**
"Colonel David Crockett was one of the most remarkable men of the times in which he lived. Born in humble life, but gifted with a strong will, an indomitable courage, and unremitting perseverance...   Biographies/New Age Pages 424

☐ **Lip-Reading** by *Edward Nitchie*   ISBN: *1-59462-206-X*   **$25.95**
Edward B. Nitchie, founder of the New York School for the Hard of Hearing, now the Nitchie School of Lip-Reading, Inc, wrote "LIP-READING Principles and Practice". The development and perfecting of this meritorious work on lip-reading was an undertaking...   How-to Pages 400

☐ **A Handbook of Suggestive Therapeutics, Applied Hypnotism, Psychic Science**   ISBN: *1-59462-214-0*   **$24.95**
by *Henry Munro*   Health/New Age/Health/Self-help Pages 376

☐ **A Doll's House: and Two Other Plays** by *Henrik Ibsen*   ISBN: *1-59462-112-8*   **$19.95**
Henrik Ibsen created this classic when in revolutionary 1848 Rome. Introducing some striking concepts in playwriting for the realist genre, this play has been studied the world over.   Fiction/Classics/Plays 308

☐ **The Light of Asia** by *sir Edwin Arnold*   ISBN: *1-59462-204-3*   **$13.95**
In this poetic masterpiece, Edwin Arnold describes the life and teachings of Buddha. The man who was to become known as Buddha to the world was born as Prince Gautama of India but he rejected the worldly riches and abandoned the reigns of power when...   Religion/History/Biographies Pages 170

☐ **The Complete Works of Guy de Maupassant** by *Guy de Maupassant*   ISBN: *1-59462-157-8*   **$16.95**
"For days and days, nights and nights, I had dreamed of that first kiss which was to consecrate our engagement, and I knew not on what spot I should put my lips..."   Fiction/Classics Pages 240

☐ **The Art of Cross-Examination** by *Francis L. Wellman*   ISBN: *1-59462-309-0*   **$26.95**
Written by a renowned trial lawyer, Wellman imparts his experience and uses case studies to explain how to use psychology to extract desired information through questioning.   How-to/Science/Reference Pages 408

☐ **Answered or Unanswered?** by *Louisa Vaughan*   ISBN: *1-59462-248-5*   **$10.95**
Miracles of Faith in China   Religion Pages 112

☐ **The Edinburgh Lectures on Mental Science (1909)** by *Thomas*   ISBN: *1-59462-008-3*   **$11.95**
This book contains the substance of a course of lectures recently given by the writer in the Queen Street Hall, Edinburgh. Its purpose is to indicate the Natural Principles governing the relation between Mental Action and Material Conditions...   New Age/Psychology Pages 148

☐ **Ayesha** by *H. Rider Haggard*   ISBN: *1-59462-301-5*   **$24.95**
Verily and indeed it is the unexpected that happens! Probably if there was one person upon the earth from whom the Editor of this, and of a certain previous history, did not expect to hear again...   Classics Pages 380

☐ **Ayala's Angel** by *Anthony Trollope*   ISBN: *1-59462-352-X*   **$29.95**
The two girls were both pretty, but Lucy who was twenty-one who supposed to be simple and comparatively unattractive, whereas Ayala was credited, as her Bombwhat romantic name might show, with poetic charm and a taste for romance. Ayala when her father died was nineteen...   Fiction Pages 484

☐ **The American Commonwealth** by *James Bryce*   ISBN: *1-59462-286-8*   **$34.45**
An interpretation of American democratic political theory. It examines political mechanics and society from the perspective of Scotsman James Bryce   Politics Pages 572

☐ **Stories of the Pilgrims** by *Margaret P. Pumphrey*   ISBN: *1-59462-116-0*   **$17.95**
This book explores pilgrims religious oppression in England as well as their escape to Holland and eventual crossing to America on the Mayflower, and their early days in New England...   History Pages 268

QTY

The Fasting Cure *by Sinclair Upton*   ISBN: *1-59462-222-1*   **$13.95**
In the Cosmopolitan Magazine for May, 1910, and in the Contemporary Review (London) for April, 1910, I published an article dealing with my experi-
ences in fasting. I have written a great many magazine articles, but never one which attracted so much attention... New Age/Self Help/Health Pages 164

Hebrew Astrology *by Sepharial*   ISBN: *1-59462-308-2*   **$13.45**
In these days of advanced thinking it is a matter of common observation that we have left many of the old landmarks behind and that we are now pressing
forward to greater heights and to a wider horizon than that which represented the mind-content of our progenitors... Astrology Pages 144

Thought Vibration or The Law of Attraction in the Thought World   ISBN: *1-59462-127-6*   **$12.95**

by William Walker Atkinson   Psychology/Religion Pages 144

Optimism *by Helen Keller*   ISBN: *1-59462-108-X*   **$15.95**
Helen Keller was blind, deaf, and mute since 19 months old, yet famously learned how to overcome these handicaps, communicate with the world, and
spread her lectures promoting optimism. An inspiring read for everyone... Biographies/Inspirational Pages 84

Sara Crewe *by Frances Burnett*   ISBN: *1-59462-360-0*   **$9.45**
In the first place, Miss Minchin lived in London. Her home was a large, dull, tall one, in a large, dull square, where all the houses were alike, and all the
sparrows were alike, and where all the door-knockers made the same heavy sound... Childrens/Classic Pages 88

The Autobiography of Benjamin Franklin *by Benjamin Franklin*   ISBN: *1-59462-135-7*   **$24.95**
The Autobiography of Benjamin Franklin has probably been more extensively read than any other American historical work, and no other book of its kind
has had such ups and downs of fortune. Franklin lived for many years in England, where he was agent... Biographies/History Pages 332

Name	
Email	
Telephone	
Address	
City, State ZIP	

☐ **Credit Card**   ☐ **Check / Money Order**

Credit Card Number	
Expiration Date	
Signature	

Please Mail to: Book Jungle
PO Box 2226
Champaign, IL 61825
or Fax to: 630-214-0564

ORDERING INFORMATION

web*: www.bookjungle.com*
email*: sales@bookjungle.com*
fax*: 630-214-0564*
mail*: Book Jungle PO Box 2226 Champaign, IL 61825*
or PayPal *to sales@bookjungle.com*

Please contact us for bulk discounts

DIRECT-ORDER TERMS

**20% Discount if You Order
Two or More Books**
Free Domestic Shipping!
Accepted: Master Card, Visa,
Discover, American Express